NIGHT AT THE MUSEUM
SECRET OF THE TOMB

A Junior Novelization

NIGHT AT THE MUSEUM
SECRET OF THE TOMB

A Junior Novelization

Written by
Michael Anthony Steele

Based on the motion picture screenplay written by David Guion and
Michael Handelman. Story by Thomas Lennon,
Robert Ben Garant, David Guion, and Michael Handelman.

BARRON'S

Written by Michael Anthony Steele
Based on the motion picture screenplay written by David Guion and Michael
Handelman. Story by Thomas Lennon, Robert Ben Garant, David Guion, and
Michael Handelman.

All inquiries should be addressed to:
Barron's Educational Series, Inc.
250 Wireless Boulevard
Hauppauge, NY 11788
www.barronseduc.com

ISBN: 978-1-4380-0524-9

Library of Congress Control Number: 2014946153

Date of Manufacture: November 2014
Manufactured by: B12V12G, Berryville, VA

Printed in the United States of America
9 8 7 6 5 4 3 2

CHAPTER 1

Larry Daley watched the line of black limousines snake up the circular drive. Soon after, men in crisp tuxedos and women in sparkling evening gowns stepped out of the sleek cars. The dazzling guests strolled up the red carpet amid a barrage of camera flashes from photographers. On each side of the carpet, large spotlights aimed their glowing beams at the night sky. The towering shafts of light crisscrossed above as everyone made their way toward the museum's north entrance. When the first of the guests reached the entryway, Larry raised a walkie-talkie to his mouth and keyed the microphone.

"The house is open," he reported. "T-minus twenty-five minutes until show time."

Larry straightened the bow tie of his own tuxedo before strolling over to Dr. McPhee. The short museum director dabbed at his forehead with a white handkerchief.

"Looking good, Dr. McPhee." Larry reached out and pinched the shiny lapel of McPhee's tuxedo jacket. "Rental?"

The director slapped his hand away. "No, it's not a rental!" He wiped at his lapel with the handkerchief. "I run a major cultural institution. I'm not some sweaty teenager at prom."

Larry smiled and followed the director toward the entrance. The guests passed under a thin arch just above the open doors. Beyond the arch, their destination was the newest wing of the Museum of Natural History.

The structure was an architectural marvel. It was essentially a huge sphere suspended inside a giant glass cube. Inside the cube, guests gathered and mingled under the hanging sphere. Later, the guests would enter the sphere itself. The large silver sphere contained the planetarium, where the bulk of the festivities would be held. The entire event was a celebration for the reopening of the museum's Center for Earth and Space.

Dr. McPhee took in a deep breath. "Excitement! The grand planetarium reopening." He gestured to the red carpet. "Lots of V-important-Ps." He shuddered. "I'm so nervous." He then shook his head. "Not really."

Larry smirked. "Yeah, you seem...calm."

McPhee raised his chin. "Simple explanation. I am." He strode through the main doors and Larry followed.

They found themselves amongst the glamorously dressed guests. Each board member and museum donor held a drink, enjoyed an appetizer, or chitchatted with one another. All of them hobnobbed under the suspended globe.

The museum director pointed out a woman with blonde hair and thick-rimmed glasses. "There she is," said McPhee. "Our new chairwoman."

Larry had only met Madeleine Phelps once before. Even though Larry worked at the museum, he rarely bumped into any of the board members. Larry Daley strictly worked the night shift.

"Huge amount of pressure on you," said McPhee. "I hope you have all the special effects wizardry in order."

Larry sighed. "Just another day at the office."

Over the years, Larry had tried to let Dr. McPhee in on the museum's secret. He tried to explain how the Egyptian artifact, the Tablet of Ahkmenrah, was magical. Not just magical in the sense that it was made of gold and sparkled brightly. It was *truly magical*. Each night, at sunset, the tablet glowed and made the museum's many exhibits come to life. Unfortunately, the museum director refused to believe it. It was almost as if he couldn't wrap his brain around the concept. Instead, McPhee insisted that Larry somehow made it all possible through ingenious special effects.

Madeleine Phelps spotted Larry and McPhee and crossed to greet them. "Good evening, gentlemen," she said.

"Ah, our esteemed chairwoman," said McPhee. He gave a curt bow and then gestured to Larry. "You remember Larry Daley, our Director of Nighttime Operations."

"Hi, Dr. Phelps," said Larry

"The museum Board owes you a debt of gratitude, Mr. Daley," said Dr. Phelps. "Your night program has boosted attendance over thirty percent."

Larry shrugged. "That's what they tell me."

"*Director* is just his title, really," explained McPhee. "He's more of a night guard, actually. I'm the *head* of the whole museum. Buck stops...and also starts...with me." He waved a dismissive hand at Larry. "Mr. Daley merely executes my grand plans."

Larry shook his head. He couldn't believe McPhee was taking all the credit. After Larry began working at the museum, he soon discovered what went on at night, when the museum was closed. It had been Larry's idea to keep the museum open into the night.

That way, the rest of the world could enjoy the living exhibits.

"You surprise me, Dr. McPhee," said Dr. Phelps. "You're a visionary! And yet, in person, you seem …not that way."

"Well, I am," said McPhee. He shrugged his shoulders and rolled his eyes. "So, debt of gratitude …mine."

Dr. Phelps leaned closer. "Tell me…the animatronic motors inside the dinosaur…how did you make them so tiny and yet so powerful?"

"Well…uh," McPhee stammered. "Mr. Daley can explain the technical details."

Dr. Phelps turned to Larry.

Larry raised both hands. "No, no. It's all Dr. McPhee, really." Larry wasn't about to let McPhee off the hook that easily.

Dr. Phelps turned back to McPhee.

"Ah. Yes. Well…a good magician…never reveals his tricks…and all that," McPhee said clumsily. "Peel away too many layers and pretty soon…no more onion."

"Well, I don't have to tell you how much effort has gone into the renovation of this planetarium," said Dr. Phelps. "It's critical that this evening go off smoothly. I sincerely hope you gentlemen are ready."

Dr. McPhee smiled. "Oh, don't worry. We were born..." The director glanced at Larry nervously.

Larry smiled. "Yes, we're ready. We were born ready."

"That's what I said. Obviously," snorted McPhee.

Dr. Phelps glanced from McPhee, to Larry, and then back to McPhee. "I'm going to go talk to other people now."

Larry was glad Dr. Phelps left. He didn't want to be rude but he really had to go check on everyone. Like she said, they had to be ready. He turned to leave.

"Oh, Mr. Daley. Have you seen the new Neanderthal exhibit?" asked McPhee. "I supervised the renovation myself. I think you'll like it." The museum director clasped his hands behind his back and strolled into the crowd.

Larry didn't know what the man was talking about. Whatever it was, it didn't matter right now. He brought the walkie-talkie to his lips and keyed the mic. "Okay, guys...twenty minutes!"

Larry moved through the service corridors and made his way to the main hall. This was the usual entrance to the Museum of Natural History and it was built to impress any and all who entered. The front doors opened to reveal a large rotunda with gleaming marble floors. Stone pillars circled the hall, holding up the second- and third-story walkways. Two large marble staircases wound up to the second floor. Normally, visitors would be greeted by several static displays, including a fossilized Tyrannosaurus Rex skeleton—whom Larry had named, Rexy. However, because it was night and the tablet's magic was doing its thing, the hall was alive with bustling, walking and talking museum exhibits.

As soon as Larry entered, Sacajawea fell into step beside him. Once, she was a Native-American scout for the famed Lewis and Clark Expedition. Now, she helped Larry get everyone ready for the big night. She wore her traditional beaded, buckskin skirt and wore her dark hair in two long black braids. She handed Larry a clipboard.

"Rexy has been waxed and buffed," she reported. "Teddy is grooming his mustache. And I've reviewed fire safety procedures with the primordial men."

"Great," replied Larry. He went over the checklist on the clipboard. "Tell the centurions to stretch. I don't want anyone pulling a hamstring."

As Sacajawea peeled away, Larry addressed the crowd of living museum exhibits.

"Guys, we've got the mayor and the governor out there," said Larry. He pumped a fist. "I need you to bring it!"

Larry ducked under Rexy's bony tail as the T-Rex skeleton lumbered past. "Rexy, watch that tail. There's going to be open flame out there."

Larry spotted a capuchin monkey in the crowd. "Dex, how you feeling?"

Dexter put one arm over his head and stretched like a gymnast. He gave a happy chirp and clapped his paws together. A puff of powdery gym chalk burst from between his tiny monkey hands.

Larry marched to the information desk. The surface was covered with tiny Roman centurions from the diorama wing. A miniature cowboy, Jedediah from the Wild West diorama, stood with them.

One of the soldiers marched across the desk toward their legion commander, Octavius. "Everything is ready, my liege!" the soldier reported.

Octavius grinned. "Then let the diversions begin!"

All at once, four centurions leaped into the air. They came down upon the computer keyboard's space bar. The screen above them came to life, revealing a video of two kittens chasing the red dot from a laser pointer.

"Doggone it," said Jed. "You can't ambush me with that kind of cute! That's not even fair!"

"I should like to comment!" announced Octavius. "Summon the apparatus!"

A nearby sentry turned and cupped his hands around his mouth. "Summon the apparatus!" he shouted.

At once, several centurions wheeled in a large wooden device. A cross between a catapult and a modern-day piece of construction equipment, the apparatus fit perfectly over the computer keyboard. A lone centurion sat on a tiny seat in the center of the structure.

"L!" shouted Octavius.

The centurion spun wheels and pulled levers until a large ice cream stick struck the *L* key on the keyboard.

"O! L!" continued Octavius.

The centurion operated the controls until the *O* and *L* keys were struck.

"Now post this video and my edict of approval to Facebook!" ordered Octavius.

"Shall I prepare your Twitter, my liege?" asked the centurion.

Jed took off his cowboy hat and slapped it against his thigh. "Are you crazy?" he asked. "This ain't no time for indiscriminate tweetin'! This here's just for our friends…and people we vaguely recall from childhood."

Larry shook his head and sighed. "Come on, guys. Let's focus on the show. Don't make me change the password again."

As Larry prepared to check on the rest of the group, Teddy Roosevelt, twenty-sixth president of the United States, rode up on his horse. He wore his tan Rough Rider uniform complete with a wide-brimmed hat, a glistening saber, and long leather gloves.

"Teddy, are we ready to roll?" asked Larry.

The former president displayed his typical wide grin under his bushy mustache. "Yes indeed, Lawrence." He climbed off his horse and stepped closer. "But...have you seen the Neanderthals lately?"

"No," replied Larry. "Why is everybody talking about this?"

Teddy cringed and gestured to the south side of the hall. "You might want to take a look."

With Teddy in tow, Larry marched over to the huddled group of hairy cavemen. "Hey guys. What's up?" asked Larry.

One by one, they each turned to face him. They each had protruding jaws, low brows, and dull eyes. When the last one turned, Larry understood what Teddy wanted him to see. There was a new Neanderthal in the museum. And this particular figure was created to look like a caveman version of Larry himself.

"Great," Larry muttered. "Thank you, Dr. McPhee."

"You could choose to look at it as a very nice tribute," suggested Teddy.

Larry nodded. "Right." He turned his attention to the new arrival. "Hi, there." Larry tapped his own chest. He knew how to talk to these guys. "I'm Larry."

The Neanderthal cocked his head and gave a puzzled expression. Then he mimicked Larry's gesture and tapped his chest. "Laaa..." said the caveman in a raspy voice.

Larry frowned. "Okay. Hi...Laaa." He glanced at Teddy. The former president merely shrugged. Larry turned back to...Laaa. "Anyway..." Larry tapped his own chest again. "Larry. Nice to meet you."

Laaa reached out and grabbed Larry's face with one hand. He felt his nose, his hair, and his lips. Then the caveman repeated the motions, feeling his own face with his other hand. He leaned forward and looked Larry in the eyes. "Dada?" asked Laaa.

"Nope." Larry quickly shook his head. "Not your Dada."

Laaa's face broke into a wide, toothy grin. He threw his arms around Larry, giving him a crushing hug. "Dada!"

Larry winced at the pain of the embrace. Not to mention the smell. "Again, no. Not Dada."

11

"Dum-Dum got a new son-son!" said a booming voice. Larry cut his eyes to see the giant Easter Island Head chuckling.

"Okay, I don't have time for this right now," said Larry. He pulled himself from the hairy hug and marched away.

"I actually found that quite touching," said Teddy as he followed.

Larry and Teddy moved up one of the marble staircases to the second floor walkway.

"Well, Lawrence, tonight is our collective chance to shine," said Teddy. "I want you to know how proud I am. Quite a feather in your capalackpagillapropper!"

Larry and Teddy froze and stared at each other.

"Are you okay, Teddy?" asked Larry.

"That was odd," said Teddy, cocking his head. "Apologies, Lawrence. Not sure what that was, I confess." His grin returned. "But yes, son. I'm fine." He gestured to the top of the stairs. "Shall we?"

They met Sacajawea on the walkway. Larry placed his hands on the rail and gazed down at the main floor. The museum's exhibits from many continents and time periods milled about. Of course, they were more than just mere exhibits—and not simply because they came to life every night. Since Larry discovered them during his first evening as a museum night guard, he had grown to care deeply for each and every one of them. Yes, they were much more than mere exhibits. They were his friends.

"All right, everybody!" shouted Larry. The crowd fell to a hush. "How are you guys feeling?"

Everyone cheered.

Larry smiled and held up his hands. When the cheers died down, he continued. "Guys, this is just like rehearsal. Only difference...five hundred extremely important people will be watching you. I don't want to stress you guys out, but Regis Philbin is even out there."

There was a ripple of nervous excitement.

"*Reejo Philbo*?" asked Attila the Hun with wide eyes. His leather armor had been polished to a high sheen. Even the horsetail jutting from his fur-trimmed hat had been neatly combed. However, the once-feared ruler of the Huns vigorously fanned himself as he took a deep, nervous breath.

Larry smiled. "Don't let it mess with your head. Don't freak out. Just relax and have fun. Who's ready to have some fun?"

The crowd cheered once more.

Teddy gave a nervous laugh. "At the battle at San Juan Hill, I was cool as a cucumber. Right now... butterflies like you wouldn't believe."

Sacajawea took his hands. "Take strength from the spirits of the Earth…and the ocean…and the four winds."

Teddy nodded and smiled.

"And if that doesn't work," she continued. "Picture the audience naked."

Larry threw a fist into the air. "Let's go!"

As everyone filed out of the main hall, Larry zipped in front of them and made his way to the Center of Earth and Space. He jogged up the winding ramp leading up to the center of the giant sphere. He stepped inside to find the guests sitting at tables in the planetarium. With the darkened dome above their heads, the VIPs enjoyed an elegant dinner.

As Larry made his way to the opposite wall, he spotted Dr. McPhee sitting at a table with Dr. Phelps and other board members. The director still tried to act casual, even though it was obvious to everyone that he was a nervous wreck.

Larry checked his watch and then held up the walkie-talkie. "Cue music," he whispered. On command, a sweeping orchestral score filled the air and the lights dimmed. Larry keyed the mic again. "And Teddy…in three, two, one…"

A spotlight snapped on, revealing Teddy Roosevelt riding his horse into the large room.
The crowd applauded.

"Since 1869, when I was a mere boy of eleven," Teddy began, "this museum has been a shining beacon to our great city. Its mission…to bring the vast sweep of history to life. All the way back to the dawn of civilization itself."

From around the room, Neanderthals entered carrying torches. The crowd muttered in amazement as the cavemen made their way through the room. They lit small lamps on each of the guests' tables.

"Tonight, we expand our horizons even further," said Teddy. "To the sun, the moon…and the stars!" He pointed to the black dome above. "Since the beginning of time, mankind has looked to the heavens and given names to what he saw. The constellations." He gave the audience a wink and smiled. "I thought you might like to meet them."

Larry keyed his mic and whispered, "And, constellations…go!"

A flash of light filled the dome and the audience gasped. Several starry figures came into view. Each one of them was made of bright points of light with a faint outline giving them shape. Leo Major, the big lion, leaped over the crowd. A starry lion cub followed him—Leo Minor. Other points of light formed the shape of a large scorpion and that of a crab—Scorpius and Cancer. The sparkling creatures used their massive claws to spar with each other, much to the crowd's delight.

"Orion the Hunter!" announced Teddy.

More stars filled the air. They swirled and then spread out to form the shape of a giant hunter with a bow and arrow.

Larry smiled as a smaller cluster of stars swirled above Dr. McPhee's head. The man looked terrified as the stars drifted into the shape of an apple. Orion jerked an arrow from his quiver and loaded his bow. Without seeming to aim, he drew back and let the arrow fly. McPhee shut his eyes as the arrow found its mark. It struck the apple, making it explode in a puff of stardust.

McPhee opened his eyes and laughed nervously. "All planned. Knew it was happening."

Teddy continued his speech. "Perhaps our primitive ancestors gazed upon these same constellations and dreamed of flight!"

"Drop the silks," Larry whispered into the radio. "And...go monkey."

Two scarlet silk banners unfurled from the ceiling. Just as they reached their full length, Dexter slid down both of them. Like a circus aerialist, he twisted and turned gracefully. He wrapped himself in the thin banners before unfurling and spinning toward the ground. Then, at the last minute, he halted between the two silks, his trembling little arms jutted out, keeping him perfectly still.

Larry smiled. "Yeah, stick it, Dex."

More stardust exploded around the monkey for his big finish. Applause erupted from the crowd.

Larry shook his head as he saw McPhee lean over to Dr. Phelps. "All me," said McPhee. "All me."

"None of this would be possible without your generosity," said Teddy. "As I look out into this crowd tonight, what do I see?"

The audience settled as Teddy paused.

The former president's smile faltered. His left eye twitched and then both eyes widened. "Invaders!" he shouted.

Larry frowned and held up the radio. "What's going on?"

Teddy leaped off his horse and landed on a nearby table. He swung his rifle around. "We're surrounded! Gather 'round, Rough Riders! We won't go down without a fight!"

The Neanderthals began to hoot, waving their torches in the air. They moved in on the audience. Above them, Dexter bared his teeth and screeched at the crowd.

Larry darted across the room toward Teddy. "Hey, folks. Little technical glitch here." He ran up to the crazed president. "Teddy, what are you doing? Stick to the script!"

Teddy wheeled around and pointed his rifle at Larry's chest.

Larry raised his hands. "Teddy. It's me."

Teddy scowled at Larry. "I don't know you!" He spun and cocked his rifle. "Remember the Maine!" He took aim and fired. A wine glass exploded across the room.

"Teddy!" shouted Larry. He jumped onto the table and twisted the rifle from the former president's grasp.

"Steady men!" shouted a tiny voice.

Larry spun to see Octavius leading a battalion of tiny soldiers and cowboys. Several of them had little lassos tied together to form long lengths of rope.

"Let's mow 'em down, fellas!" shouted Jedediah.

The miniatures spread out, stretching the ropes tight. Several fleeing guests tripped over the thin lines and tumbled to the floor.

The doors to the planetarium burst open as the rest of the exhibits poured into the room. Attila raised his sword and screamed madly as he led his Hun warriors into battle. Lions, zebras, and ostriches stampeded in. The faceless Civil War soldiers marched in and began firing their muskets into the air. More terrified guests screamed as they scattered toward the exits.

Dr. McPhee ran up to Larry. "What is this? Fix it!"

Larry didn't know where to start. His friends were going berserk. Attila used his sword to hack away at a dolphin ice sculpture. Sacajawea used a napkin as a sling to pelt audience members with hunks of cheese.

Then Larry spotted Dexter atop a tiger's back. The monkey held a long kebab skewer laden with chunks of meat and vegetables. Like a tiny general, the monkey held his spear aloft and screeched the order to charge. The tiger galloped toward Dr. Phelps' table.

"Dexter! No!" shouted Larry. He sprinted toward the table just as Dexter hurled his spear. Larry snatched the kebob from the air, the sharp tip mere inches from Dr. Phelps' face.

At the center of the pandemonium, Teddy twitched and shook. "Firgil-fliminy-geegar-zeezah!" The former president straightened, turning stiff as a board. He wobbled for a moment before falling face first into a large plate of butter.

Larry wanted to run to his friend. Unfortunately, he had something bigger to worry about—much bigger. Orion the Hunter loaded his bow with another arrow made of stars. He aimed it at the fleeing guests.

"Orion! Put the bow down!" Larry ordered.

The giant constellation released his arrow and it struck the empty tables at the center of the room.

It exploded into stardust and the tables burst into flames. Rexy came tromping through the fire, smoke and flames billowing around him. His skeletal mouth opened wide.

ROOOOOOOOOOOAAAAAAR!

Larry brought his hands to his face. "No!"

CHAPTER 2

After Larry helped put out the fires in the planetarium—both literally and figuratively—he returned to the main hall. He found all the exhibits milling around, their heads hung low. They all wore expressions of embarrassment. He marched into the middle of them.

"Guys, what was that?" Larry asked, throwing up his hands. "What were you thinking out there?"

Out of the corner of his eye, he saw his Neanderthal twin, Laaa, mimicking his movements. The caveman marched around like Larry had, throwing up his hairy arms in frustration. Larry shook his head and put a hand on the caveman's shoulder. "I've got this, Laaa," said Larry. "Go sit down."

As Laaa shuffled away, Larry rounded on Attila the Hun. "Attila, what were you doing to that dolphin?" he asked. "It's a dolphin, dude."

Attila hung his head and jutted out his lower lip in shame.

Teddy stepped forward, hat in hand. "Lawrence, my apologies. I don't know what came over us."

"Yep, sorry we ruined your hootenanny, Gigantor," said Jedediah. The tiny cowboy (who had coined the nickname for Larry years ago) stood atop a nearby display case next to Octavius.

"A thousand pardons, my liege," Octavius apologized. He slammed his fist to his bronze chest plate, making a Roman salute. "Something took hold of us like a spell."

Larry felt something warm splash onto his shoulder. He spun to see Dexter sitting atop Rexy's head. The little capuchin was peeing on him.

"Dexter, come on, man! We worked through this years ago!" Larry stepped out of the stream and pointed up to the monkey. "You know what? Fine! Tomorrow, you're in diapers like a little baby! Not cruisers! Not pull-ups! Diapers!"

Dexter covered his face with his tiny monkey hands.

"Lawrence, can't you see that this poor creature is upset?" asked Teddy. "We all are."

Larry scanned the crowd and saw what Teddy meant. His friends were not only embarrassed and ashamed, they were also frightened. It was clear that none of them knew what had come over them that night. The exhibits were clearly unnerved.

"I don't know what's going on with you guys, but that was scary tonight," said Larry. "That wasn't you."

Suddenly, a young Egyptian pharaoh swept into the main hall. "Larry! You'd better see this!"

Larry followed Ahkmenrah through the museum. Dressed in an ornate tunic and wearing a tall headpiece, the boy looked no more than eighteen years old. Larry knew differently. Ahkmenrah was actually several thousand years old. In truth, he was a mummified pharaoh from ancient Egypt. The power of his magical tablet had restored his youth as well as his life.

Larry and Ahkmenrah ran into the Egyptian wing, past two giant jackal-headed guards. The guards lowered their long spears and bowed as their king passed. The pharaoh pointed to the golden tablet hanging on a wall over Ahkmenrah's open sarcophagus.

The Tablet of Ahkmenrah was about the size of a large book. It was made up of nine moveable tiles. Different Egyptian hieroglyphic symbols were carved onto each tile. Normally, the solid gold tablet sparkled under the display lights. Now, however, it was dull and flat. A small green stain had formed on the bottom of the tablet. It almost looked like green rust. Larry didn't understand. Gold didn't tarnish like that.

"Have you ever seen it like this before?" asked Larry.

Ahkmenrah shook his head. "Never. It's always been exactly the same. This corrosion...it's never happened before." He sighed. "To be honest, my father knew the secrets of the tablet better than I did. Unfortunately, he swore he'd never reveal them. And he never did."

Larry leaned closer and studied the green stain. For a split second, the tablet cast a green glow and the stain crept an inch up the tablet.

Ahkmenrah placed a hand on Larry's shoulder to steady himself. The young man swayed slightly.

"You okay?" asked Larry.

Ahkmenrah blinked and shook his head. "Yes ...I'm fine."

"Okay, you know what? It's been a long night," said Larry. "Let's pack it in early. Tomorrow I'm going to find out what's going on here."

Larry made sure that everyone returned to his or her places in the museum before catching a cab outside. Normally, he would've stayed until sunrise, when everyone became lifeless exhibits once more. However, his friends were so upset over what had happened, they agreed to remain in their display areas until he could figure things out.

Larry arrived at his apartment building and stepped inside. As he entered the elevator, two police officers followed him in. Larry pressed the button for his floor and glanced up at the flanking men.

"Everything good?" asked Larry.

"Noise complaint," replied one of the officers.

The other police officer gave a big yawn. "Night shift, man," he said.

Larry chuckled. "Tell me about it."

They reached Larry's floor and he stepped out of the elevator. He was surprised to see that the officers followed him out. He supposed the complaint came from his floor. Then, as Larry walked down the long corridor, he heard the thumping beat of dance music. He felt a lump in his throat as he guessed the music's source. As he stepped up to his door, the floor vibrated under his feet. The music came from the other side. Larry glanced back and, sure enough, the police officers stood on either side of him. They smiled.

Larry fished out his keys. "I'll just…" He opened his apartment door and was assaulted by a wall of sound. His apartment was crowded with sweaty teenagers dancing to the thumping beat. There were so many kids in there that he could barely see his apartment.

Larry stood in shock for a moment. Then he waved his hands over his head. "All right. Party's over!" shouted Larry. Unfortunately, he couldn't be heard over the loud music. Everyone ignored him and continued dancing.

Larry spotted his son, Nick, on the far side of the living room. The seventeen-year-old wore large headphones over his shaggy dark hair. He hovered over his open laptop while bobbing his head to the beat. He was the party's DJ.

Larry navigated his way through the bouncing teenagers. He joined Nick at the DJ table and yanked a cord out of his son's computer. The music died.

Nick's head jerked up in surprise. "Dad? What are you doing here? It's three o'clock."

"Yeah, it's three o'clock," said Larry.

"Okay, everybody! Party's over!" shouted one of the officers. "Clear out. Quietly!"

The kids grumbled as they slowly made their way toward the door. Larry was about to lay into Nick when a young girl stepped between them. The auburn-haired girl pulled out a marker and wrote her name and number on Nick's arm.

"See you tomorrow night, Nick?" the girl asked.

Larry leaned forward. "Probably not." He gave her a mocking wave.

The girl frowned and followed the rest of the kids out of the apartment. Larry watched them go and waved at the police officers. "Thank you, officers. Get some rest."

Larry shook his head as he scanned his now filthy apartment. He grabbed a trash bag from the kitchen and began throwing away half-empty soda bottles and chip bags.

"I didn't know you were coming home early," said Nick.

"No kidding," Larry replied. He gestured to the mess around him. "Why would you think this is okay?"

"When I'm not at Mom's, you leave me alone every night," replied Nick. He helped his father clean up. "What did you expect?"

Larry's lips tightened. "Honesty. That's what I'd expect." He swept a pile of candy wrappers into the trash. "So what...you're a big DJ now? Throwing parties every night?"

"No, this was the first time," said Nick. He unplugged cables from his computer.

A noise from the back of the apartment caught their attention. Nick's friend, Josh, emerged from the bathroom. Josh flicked his head to the side, whisking his long bangs out of his eyes. Josh gave a fist bump to Nick. "Best party yet, dude!"

27

Larry frowned at his son. Nick smiled nervously. "This was...definitely one of the first times," said Nick.

"And that's saying a lot," Josh continued. "Because you've thrown a *lot* of parties."

Larry sighed and shook his head. "Thank you, Josh."

Josh grinned up at Larry. "Seriously, your son is an incredible host. He takes care of us...anticipates our every need."

Larry placed a hand on Josh's back. He guided the young boy toward the front door. "Josh, you've served your purpose. You can leave now." He ushered him into the hallway.

Josh turned and smiled. "Copy you, L.D."

Larry shut the door and glared at Nick. "So *this* is why you couldn't come to the museum tonight?"

"Dad, Andrea Moreno was here," Nick explained.

"Who's Andrea Moreno?" asked Larry.

Nick held up his arm revealing Andrea's name and phone number. "You just kicked her out."

Larry shook his head. "So, the point is...you lied to me."

Nick sighed. "Yes. We've established that. Let's not linger in that dark place. Let's talk about the *why*." He pointed to his arm. "Andrea Moreno. You saw her. Incredibly hot. Crazy smart. We finally had a chance to connect here tonight. And I'm going to jeopardize that just to go to your planetarium thing?"

"There was a time I couldn't get you out of the museum," said Larry. He smiled as he remembered all the adventures that he and Nick had shared there.

"There was also a time I liked riding a tricycle in the park," said Nick. He coiled up a long cable. "How'd it go tonight, by the way?"

"Don't change the subject by pretending to be interested," snapped Larry.

Nick held up his hands. "Okay, okay."

Larry sagged. "It was pretty much a disaster." He pulled two more soda bottles from between the couch cushions. "Listen, you can't be doing this right now. You have finals coming up. You have your NYU application due in two weeks..."

"I'm not going to get into NYU," Nick interrupted.

"You don't know that," said Larry.

Nick nodded. "I do...in the sense that I don't intend to apply."

Larry stopped cleaning. "What are you talking about?"

Nick shrugged. "I just don't know if it's the right place for me."

"Okay, so you want to spread your wings a bit, try somewhere outside the city," said Larry. "So where are you thinking? Let's hear the list."

Nick gave a weak smile. "It's a short list."

"No shame in a short list," said Larry. "Hit me."

"It's super short." Nick cringed. "There are zero things on it."

"Zero?" asked Larry.

"I've changed my mind about college," Nick explained. "I want to take some time off. Do what you just said. Spread my wings."

"I meant spread your wings to fly to a different school," said Larry. "I thought we had a plan."

"Yeah, well, plans change," said Nick.

"Not when your parents are paying for the plan," said Larry. "Then any plan changes have to be approved by the financiers of the plan."

"Dad ..." Nick began.

Larry raised his hand to cut him off. He put his hands on his hips and stared at his son. Larry opened his mouth to argue but nothing came out. He just had the worst night of his life and came home to find that his son, whom he had trusted to be home alone, has been throwing parties practically every night while Larry was at work.

"Dad, it's late," said Nick. "We owe it to ourselves to call it a night. Don't we?

Larry shook his head. "This conversation isn't over."

The next morning, after Nick had gone to school, Larry headed back to the museum. He saw all of his friends, frozen in the daylight hours, just as they should be. It was like nothing had ever happened. But something terrible had happened and Larry had to figure out why.

He made his way downstairs to the museum archives. The large musty room was lined with shelves filled with old artifacts and file boxes. After some digging, Larry pulled out a box containing information about the Tablet of Ahkmenrah.

He unpacked the box on a wooden table. He spread out maps, old photographs, and handwritten notes about the original expedition that discovered Ahkmenrah's tomb. While going through the material, Larry could almost picture the night the archeologists found the site. They discovered the tablet and several sarcophagi containing the remains of Ahkmenrah and his family. There had also been a strange curse—a warning that none of the archeologists had heeded. The warning was, if the tomb is disturbed, *the end will come*. Larry wondered if that meant the end of the world, like so many other ancient civilizations' warnings. Or perhaps it meant the end of the *magic* would come.

As for Ahkmenrah's family, Larry knew that the young pharaoh had an older brother—Kahmunrah. He'd had the unfortunate pleasure of making his acquaintance when Larry and several other exhibits were at the Smithsonian, in Washington D.C. But that was not who Larry was looking for. Ahkmenrah said that only his *father* knew the secret of the tablet. After some more investigating, Larry discovered that the young pharaoh's parents had been shipped to the British Museum in England.

Larry packed up the files and headed back upstairs. He dashed to Dr. McPhee's office. He found the door ajar and McPhee busy pulling diplomas from his wall. He packed the framed documents into a cardboard box.

"What's going on?" asked Larry.

"Our esteemed chairwoman has asked for my resignation," replied McPhee. "She said since the night program was my brainchild, the buck starts and stops with me."

Larry plopped down in a chair. "I'm sorry. It's my fault."

McPhee waved him away. "No, no it's my fault. *I* apologize." He packed away some more personal items. "I apologize for putting you in an inappropriately elevated position where you could burn down the planetarium and ruin my life."

"Well...it didn't really *burn* down," said Larry.

"Now we're quibbling over ways to describe different amounts of burning?" asked McPhee. "Lovely."

"I'm really sorry," said Larry.

"The capuchin was mere inches from stabbing Dr. Phelps in the face!" McPhee held up a sharp letter opener to drive his point home. "He had bloodlust in his black monkey eyes, Mr. Daley! A deep and unfathomable bloodlust!"

The former museum director sighed and tossed the letter opener into an open box. "Oh, well. This too shall pass." He shrugged. "Not my being fired. That's permanent."

Larry got to his feet. "I can fix this."

McPhee raised an eyebrow. "How?"

"I need to take the tablet and Ahkmenrah to London," said Larry.

"Sorry, processing..." McPhee waved his fingers on either side of his head. "I just explained that your shenanigans cost me my job. And you want to take two priceless artifacts with you on vacation to a foreign country?"

Larry leaned across the desk. "Listen to me. You and I both know there's something...magical about this place."

McPhee shook his head. "Not this again. It's not magic. It's special effects."

"How could it be special effects? I'm a security guard." Larry laughed. "I have no training whatsoever in computer-generated effects. There's no equipment anywhere!"

McPhee rolled his eyes. "I don't claim to understand it."

"You don't understand it because you're *afraid* to understand it." Larry tapped his head. "Because it would turn your mind inside out, man!"

Dr. McPhee stared at Larry across the desk. A glint of fear shown in his eyes. Larry hoped the director was buying it this time.

"The sun goes down. The tablet glows," Larry explained. "And everything comes to life!"

"The tablet starts to *glow*?" McPhee scoffed. "Now I *know* you're crazy."

"Listen to me. Nobody loves this place more than we do. If you don't help me, everything that's special about it might stop. And it may never come back." Larry gave a weak smile. "I'm not asking you to understand. I'm asking you to trust me."

"Mr. Daley...I want to help you," McPhee said with a smile. "But I don't work here anymore."

Larry's own smile widened. "The British Museum doesn't know that."

Dr. McPhee raised an eyebrow.

Soon after, McPhee was on the phone to the British Museum. "Yes, the mummy and the tablet both," McPhee explained. "A typical preservation job...touch 'em up, shine 'em up." There was a pause as someone on the other end spoke. "Yes, I'm sending my top man, Larry Daley. Under my authority as head of the museum...which I still am." There was another pause. "Righto," answered McPhee. He hung up the phone and turned to Larry. "You're in."

Larry zipped home, packed some bags, and headed over to Nick's school. He spotted his son as the boy left the building with a couple of his friends.

"Nicky!" shouted Larry. He ran across the street to catch up with the boy.

Nick's friends peeled away as Nick shook his head. "What are you doing here?" his son asked.

"I need to talk to you," said Larry.

"You couldn't just text me from someplace where no one could see you?" asked Nick.

Larry rolled his eyes. "I don't want to be seen with you either, but we have talk. We're going to London. Tonight."

"What? I can't go to London," said Nick. "I have school."

"School isn't important. Forget school," said Larry.

Nick laughed. "Okay...excellent parenting."

"You can miss a few days," Larry explained. "Your mom's out of town and obviously after last night, I'm not going to leave you..."

Larry was interrupted by the sound of someone delivering a massive karate chop—*Hi-yah!* It was Nick's phone. The sound indicated that someone had just sent Nick a text. Nick pulled out his phone and began to text back.

"Hey, can you not do that right now..." Larry began to ask. But before Larry could finish, Nick had already sent his reply.

Larry was still surprised by his son's texting speed. He shook his head, trying to finish his train of thought. "Look, this will be good," Larry continued. "Remember how we were going to do that father-son bonding trip? Drive across the country? This is like that, but better."

"I didn't want to do that," said Nick.

"What are talking about?" Larry asked, taken aback. "You were super disappointed."

"No, you said you couldn't go because of work," Nick explained. "So I acted super disappointed. Everybody wins."

Now it was Larry's turn to be disappointed—but for real. "Okay…I thought you really wanted to do that."

"Dad, I can't go," said Nick. "I'm busy."

"With what? Planning your next year doing nothing?" asked Larry. "Come on, you said you wanted an adventure. This is it."

"When did I ever say I wanted an adventure?" asked Nick.

Larry's lips tightened. "Look, this is what's happening, okay?"

"So the outcome of this conversation was decided before we started?" asked Nick.

Larry took a deep breath. "Nick, the guys are in trouble. I'm your dad, and you're coming with me."

CHAPTER 3

After an eight-hour flight, Larry and Nick watched as the large wooden crate was loaded into the rental truck—or rental *lorry*, as it was called in England. Once everything was secured, Larry drove the truck into the heart of London, toward the British Museum. The occasional black taxi swerved and honked at him. Larry had a tough time getting used to driving on the left side of the road.

Along the way, Larry parked the truck and hopped out. They had some time to see a couple of sights before their mission began. He zipped up his overcoat against the chilly London air.

"We'll head over to the museum after sundown," announced Larry. He glanced up at the late afternoon sun. "In about ninety minutes."

Nick climbed out after him. "You can tell that by looking?"

Larry smiled. "It's what I do."

Father and son walked along a sidewalk overlooking the famous Thames River. Larry didn't just want to see the sights. He wanted to talk to Nick about their discussion from the night before. Unfortunately, he had trouble getting started.

It used to be so much easier to talk to his son. When Nick was younger, he and Larry had similar interests. They spent most of their time together in the museum with all their historical friends. They even used to enjoy discovering new things about history together. Granted, usually they were looking up a historical fact to solve the occasional crisis at the museum. But no matter why they did it, they enjoyed doing it together.

But now that Nick was older, his interests had changed. He was dating, listening to new kinds of music, and spending less and less time at the museum. That meant spending less time with his father, too. Sometimes Larry felt as if he lived with a young roommate instead of a son.

Deep in his heart, Larry knew that this was all normal for his son and just part of growing up. But knowing that fact didn't make it any less painful as he and his son drifted apart.

Larry stopped and pointed to a large bridge. A tall brick tower protruded from each end of the majestic structure.

"Tower of London," said Larry. "That's where Mary Queen of Scots was executed."

"That's the Tower Bridge," Nick corrected. He pointed to the pale brick castle with four corner towers jutting toward the sky. "*That's* the Tower of London. And it was Anne Boleyn."

Larry nodded, knowingly. "All happened right around here." He patted his son on the shoulder. "Very historic region."

They started moving again. After a few steps, Larry decided to go for it.

"So, let's talk about this year off," said Larry. "Could be cool. What are you thinking?"

Nick rubbed the back of his head. "Yeah, I was thinking I might like to do something with music."

"Okay, great," said Larry. "Are we building on those two years of violin from middle school?" The image of Nick in a tuxedo came to mind. He imagined his son playing a violin solo in front of a full orchestra.

"Well, no," said Nick. "I'm coming at it more from the...DJ angle."

"Okay..." The image of Nick in a tuxedo vanished.

Nick smiled. "I want to DJ in Ibiza." He pronounced it *ibeetha*.

"In a what?" asked Larry.

"Ibiza," Nick repeated. "It's an island off the coast of Spain. That's how you pronounce it."

Larry's brow furrowed as he nodded. "Okay, right, sure."

"My friend's cousin is a club promoter. He lives in Majorca." Nick's eyes lit up. "He said we could crash with him. There's a huge party scene. A lot of great DJs come out of there." He began counting on his fingers. "DJ Beelzebub, DJ Side Salad..."

Larry wanted to ask him what he was thinking. He wanted to tell his son it was the craziest idea he had ever heard. However, he wanted to be supportive and hear him out. So all Larry said was, "Okay..."

"Dad, you didn't go to college," said Nick.

Larry stopped walking. "Wait, now we're talking about not going to college at all?"

Nick shrugged. "I'm just saying...you turned out relatively fine."

"Thank you," said Larry. "I think."

Nick smiled. "My point is...you're happy."

Larry winced. "Yeah, but it took...twenty years and a dozen career failures to get there."

"But now you're doing what you love," said Nick.

"Yeah, Nick...there aren't a lot of job openings at magical museums where everything comes to life at night," Larry explained. He held up his thumb and forefinger. "Real small bull's-eye for that one."

"Dad, whatever," Nick rolled his eyes and started walking again. "It's not going to be your problem anymore."

Larry took his son's arm. "Nicky, you're always going to be my problem."

Nick pulled his arm free. "Nice."

"Come on, Nick," said Larry. "You know what I mean."

Nick nodded. "Sun's going down. Shouldn't we head over?"

"Yeah." Larry sighed. "By the way, can you drive a stick?"

Just before sunset, Larry and Nick pulled up to the British Museum's rear gate. The large museum was closed for the day and only a lone night guard occupied a small guard station in the back. The little shed sat in front of a chain-link gate and had a small window facing the narrow road leading through to the building. Nick ducked down as Larry pulled up next to the small building.

Inside the shack sat a young woman wearing a guard uniform and oversized pieces of jewelry. Her blonde hair was pulled back in a ponytail. A name badge was pinned to the lapel of her guard uniform. Her name was Tilly.

"No, Tarquin, you're not understanding me, luv," Tilly said. The woman held a cell phone in one hand and twirled a long strand of her chewing gum with the other. "You're not listening."

Larry pulled to a stop next to the window. He put the truck in park and gave Tilly a small wave. "Hi."

The woman cut her eyes to Larry. "Sorry, Tarquin. Strange man here. Ring you later." The British Museum night guard switched off her phone, popped the gum back into her mouth, and leaned out the window. She gestured to the truck. "What's this then?"

Larry waved again. "Hi. Larry Daley. I have a delivery from Natural History in New York. For your Conservation Department." He handed over the paperwork Dr. McPhee had printed out before they left.

The guard took the papers and scanned them. She looked Larry over, noticing his guard uniform. "They let you travel?" she asked. "Must be nice being a security guard in America."

Larry shrugged and grinned. "Well, this is kind of unusual."

The guard smacked her gum. "They let me travel. You know where? Home. Here. Back home again."

Larry nodded. "Yeah, I hear ya."

"I don't even get to go inside," she continued. "Every night I come to one of the finest museums in the world and I sit outside in a box." Tilly stretched her gum into a long strand again and began twirling again. "Look at my shack. It's a bloody stand-alone. It doesn't even touch the building." She popped her gum back in and leaned farther out the window. "And do I get a weapon? Oh, no." She gestured at Larry. "You probably get a super sleek handgun with a silencer on it and everything."

Larry shook his head. "I...I don't have a weapon. No."

Tilly rolled her eyes. "That's what they all say." She leaned back into the shack. "You know what I get?" She held up a small hammer in mock pride. "Issued to me for, and I quote, *minor repairs and beautifications*." She waved the hammer over her head. "To the shack, naturally." She leaned out again. "You catch a lot of criminals, then?"

"Uh...not really," Larry replied. "Well, a couple. Back when I first started."

Tilly's eyes widened. "Wow, jazzy." She glanced around. "You know how many baddies I've killed?"

Larry shook his head.

"Zero. Nada," she said. "Why? Because England is a civilized country. We don't go around robbing museums left and right like in America where it's the national pastime."

Larry grimaced. "Okay...that's not even a little bit true." He pointed over his shoulder. "Anyway, if we're good, I'll just leave this..."

"Hold on there, world traveler, crime-fighter," Tilly interrupted. "I'll just call your museum to confirm." She scanned the paperwork and punched numbers into the guard shack's speakerphone.

"Not really necessary," Larry explained. He pointed to the papers. "It's confirmed already. See?"

Tilly's eyes narrowed. "In England, we *double* confirm."

Larry tensed as he heard the phone ringing through the small speaker. Then he relaxed as a familiar voice answered. "Dr. McPhee here."

"British Museum, sir," said Tilly. "Confirming a delivery to our conservation department."

"Yes, I signed the paperwork," replied McPhee. "Now, I can't be chatting on the phone all day. I have a museum to run after all." There was a click as he hung up the phone.

Larry breathed easier.

"Right," said Tilly. She stepped out of her guard shack and walked behind the chain gate.

Larry made sure he held up his smart phone as she punched in the security code to the keypad. After he heard the four tones, the gate unlocked and she slid it open. Larry drove through and backed the truck up to one of the loading docks. He hopped out and followed Tilly inside. With the help of a floor dolly, the two hauled the large wooden crate out of the truck and into the freight room.

"Thanks a lot," said Larry. He headed outside as she closed up the loading bay doors. By the time Tilly came outside, all she would see was Larry's arm waving from the driver's window as the truck pulled out of the gate. That's exactly what Larry wanted her to see. As Tilly made her way back to the guard shack, Larry concealed himself next to the building. It had really been Nick driving the truck.

Staying to the shadows, Larry waited until the amber rays of the sun dipped below the horizon. In that instant, the golden glow of the tablet's activation emanated through the windows of the British Museum's freight room. Larry could barely make out the sound of Ahkmenrah stirring to life inside the crate. It was GO time.

Larry snuck over to the gate. He could hear Tilly back on the phone, arguing with her boyfriend. Larry dug his phone from his pocket and pulled up the app that recorded the tones from the access panel. The app told him exactly what numbers the tones had been; he had the security code. As he entered the numbers, he spotted Nick sneaking toward him. His son ducked under the guard shack window and shuffled over to the gate. Larry slid it open just enough for his son to pass through.

"I'm not a legal expert, but this is feeling sort of international felony-ish," whispered Nick.

"You're right," Larry whispered. He slid the gate shut behind his son. "You're not a legal expert." He led the way as they crept toward the back entrance.

Nick shook his head. "Okay, but *you're* calling mom from jail."

Once at the door, Larry gave it two soft knocks. The door opened slightly and Ahkmenrah appeared on the other side. The young pharaoh held the golden tablet. Larry glanced at the guard shack one last time before he and Nick slipped inside.

"Thanks, Ahk," said Larry. He gave Nick's back a pat. "Let's go."

Ahkmenrah gave a weak smile. "Larry, the others felt…perhaps we could use some help."

Larry stopped in his tracks. "What do you mean, *the others?*" He turned and saw Teddy Roosevelt climb over the edge of the open packing crate behind them.

"You couldn't expect me to sit idly by," said the former president. He brushed packing peanuts off his uniform. "Our very survival is at stake."

Larry wasn't expecting anyone but Ahkmenrah to join him and Nick on their trip to England. But, then again, what was one more? "Good idea," agreed Larry. He nodded toward the former president. "Teddy. A good man to have in a crisis."

Larry was surprised to see Attila the Hun sit up amid a burst of foam peanuts. The large warrior followed Teddy out of the crate.

Larry sighed. "Okay…a little muscle never hurts."

Teddy reached past the Hun and took the slender hand of Sacajawea. "Wonderful tracking abilities," said Teddy. He helped the Native-American woman out of the crate. "Not to mention a deep emotional companionship that becomes richer and more fulfilling with each passing day." He brought her hand to his lips and gave it a tender kiss.

Larry rolled his eyes. "Very romantic."

A few more packing peanuts burst from the crate. Then four tiny hands appeared on the lip of the open container. Jed and Octavius hauled themselves up to the edge.

Larry shook his head. "Not totally necessary. But …you guys can do recon…I guess."

Suddenly, Dexter burst from the open crate in an explosion of packing peanuts. The mischievous monkey landed on the rim and grinned up at everyone.

Larry turned to Teddy. "You want to walk me through the thinking here?"

"I actually tied him in a sock and locked him in McPhee's filing cabinet," explained Teddy. "He's some kind of Houdini monkey."

Dexter wasn't the last to exit. A hairy hand reached out and grabbed the edge. Laaa, Larry's Neanderthal twin, pulled himself out of the wooden box. The caveman's eyes widened when he spotted Larry. "Dada!"

Larry's lips tightened. "No possible benefit whatsoever."

Ahkmenrah's face softened. "He really wanted to come."

Laaa stumbled out of the crate and stood facing Nick. Laaa eyed the boy suspiciously.

"Laaa, this is my son, Nick," said Larry. "My *actual* son."

"Hi," said Nick. He reached out to shake Laaa's hand. The Neanderthal only glared at the boy.

Teddy clasped his gloved hands together. "All right, Lawrence. What's the plan of attack?"

Larry addressed his circle of friends. "Basically, we need to get to the Egyptian Wing. Hopefully Ahk's dad can help fix whatever's wrong with the tablet."

Larry glanced around his circle of friends. Laaa wasn't there. Instead, he stood by the crate, staring at them while he munched on a handful of packing peanuts as if they were movie-theater popcorn.

Larry shook his head and marched over to the caveman. "Okay, you know what, Laaa? I would love to bring you with the rest of us. But I've got a super important job for you. Come over here."

Laaa dropped the peanuts and followed Larry. Laaa shot Nick a triumphant look as he and Larry moved toward the door leading outside.

Larry pointed to the metal door. "I want you to watch this door. Make sure nothing comes in or out. Seal it up tight. You're going to be a guard...just like me."

Laaa stared blankly at Larry.

Larry glanced at the others. "Is he getting this?"

Teddy shook his head. "I don't believe so. No."

"Not a word," added Sacajawea.

Larry pointed to the door again. "Nobody comes in. Nobody goes out." He pointed to the ground. "Stay."

Laaa nodded. "Staaaay."

"Good." Larry patted the caveman's shoulder. Then Larry turned to join the others. Unfortunately, Laaa followed him back.

"No, Laaa." Larry shook his head. He pointed back to the door. "Stay."

Laaa grinned and nodded vigorously. "Staaaay!"

"Okay, no," said Larry. He took the Neanderthal's arm and led him back to the door. "Come here."

Larry grabbed Laaa's hands and placed them flat on the door. "Hands here. Okay? No move."

Laaa glanced at both of his hands and finally seemed to get it. He grunted and smiled at Larry.

"Good. Stay there." Larry slowly backed away. "We'll come back for you. Stay."

"Staaaay," Laaa repeated. He stared intently at his hands on the door.

Seeing that Laaa finally wasn't going anywhere, Larry swept past the others. He headed toward a set of double doors at the other side of the freight room. Nick and the exhibits from New York fell into step behind him.

Larry stopped at the doors and turned to the others. "Listen up," he said. "This place is waking up for the first time. Stay together. We have no idea what's out there."

He pushed through the doors and entered a large dark chamber. The others slowly followed. Eerie scraping sounds filled the air and dark shadows moved around them. Strange howls and cries sounded in the distance.

Attila's wide eyes darted around. "Magga kalaskaa," he whispered.

"I know, big guy," said Larry. "It's spooky, all right." He gave the Hun a reassuring pat on the shoulder. "Just stay close."

As Larry's eyes adjusted to darkness, he could make out some of the misshapen figures around them. They seemed to be living statues. Suddenly, three marble women lurched into a shaft of light ahead of them. They were stark white and wore long flowing togas. Under normal circumstances, their appearance wouldn't be so frightening. However, the three living statues were missing different body parts. One was even headless. The two with heads turned to them and trained their blank, unblinking eyes at the new arrivals.

Jed and Octavius peered out from the fur rim of Attila's hat. "What kind of haunted hootenanny is this?" asked Jed.

"These figures are from the Parthenon," replied Octavius. "Before my time. Ancient Greece."

"We're all finding this super creepy, right?" said Nick.

Nick was right. The group from New York suddenly found themselves surrounded by shambling misshapen figures. A disfigured centaur hobbled closer. Disembodied arms dragged themselves forward. Headless figures reached for them with fingerless hands. Larry felt as if he were in the middle of a scary zombie movie.

"They're probably just a little freaked out," Larry explained.

"The first time we woke up . . ." added Teddy. "Well, being alive took some getting used to."

A muscular statue hobbled into the center of the surrounding figures. The stone man was missing both hands and his legs were stumped at the knees. He scraped the marble floor as he dragged himself closer, reaching up toward Larry. He looked like a statue of a wrestler.

"Oh, hey," said Larry, smiling down at the marble man. "We don't want any trouble. We're just trying to get to Egypt."

With shocking speed, the statue dove for Larry's legs. The wrestler landed on the floor and slid along the marble on his belly. Without even thinking, Larry performed an old wrestling move he remembered. He dove onto the back of the statue. With his stomach pinned to the statue's back, he spun around. He slid back and landed on his feet behind the wrestler.

Nick's eyes widened. "What the heck was that?"

Larry stayed in a crouch as he faced the statue. "I wrestled 148 in high school."

"Really?" Nick raised an eyebrow. "I never knew that."

Larry nodded. "Yeah, man. Third place in the Kings County regionals."

The stone wrestler struggled to rise. Unfortunately, his broken appendages couldn't get any traction on the smooth floor.

Larry felt sorry for the wrestler. At one time, the statue would have represented all the strength and power of the popular Greek sport.

"It's all right," said Larry. He knelt beside the figure. "Slippery floor and no...appendages. Tough. I get it."

The wrestler jerked and a stone leg flew in from nowhere. It struck Larry's legs, knocking him off his feet. In a flash, the wrestler statue was all over the night guard. He wrapped his thick thighs around Larry's head and squeezed.

Larry beat at the floor with one open palm. "Dude! I'm tapping out!" He cut his eyes up to Teddy. "How do you say tapping out in Latin?"

"Dad," said Nick.

Larry looked over at Nick. "What?" he could barely ask as the clamping legs tightened around his neck.

"Foot," replied his son.

Nick slid a marble foot across the floor. It came to a stop just a few inches from Larry's face. The stone toes wiggled.

Teddy smiled. "Make him whole, son."

"What?" asked Larry. He felt dizzy from the lack of oxygen to his brain.

"The mightiest redwood is only as strong as its roots, Lawrence," replied Teddy.

Larry reached a free hand and snatched up the foot. "You want the foot?" he asked the wrestler. Larry held up the foot. It had a metal rod sticking out of the top. The wrestler's grip loosened just enough for Larry to slip the rod into the slot inside one of the statue's ankles. The wrestler released Larry and examined his new foot he flexed it and smiled.

"Good?" asked Larry. "You like that? Want another one?"

The wrestler nodded as he stood and hopped on his new foot. Sacajawea handed Larry another foot. Larry crouched and carefully fit the second foot onto the wrestler's other ankle.

"Here you go," said Larry. "Nice arch support in there." He stood and motioned to the statue. "Walk around on it. See how it feels." Larry felt like a shoe salesman.

The wrestler propped himself up on his new feet. He walked in a small circle before charging at Larry once more.

"Whoah!" Larry threw up his arms and backed away.

Instead of trapping Larry in another wrestling hold, the statue wrapped his arms around Larry and lifted him off the ground with a hug of gratitude.

When the statue finally released him, Larry smiled at his friends. "Come on, let's help these guys out."

Larry snatched up a crawling hand and placed it on the broken wrist of a man wearing a toga. Teddy and Sacajawea scooped up arms and legs and passed them out among the statues. Nick was thanked with a wide smile when he placed a woman's head onto a statue's headless body. With everyone's help, replacement limbs were found for all the Parthenon statues. Granted, they weren't all perfect fits, but none of the Greek exhibits seemed to mind.

"Manda go soon daaah!" said Attila. He placed a horse's head onto a headless woman.

"Uh..." Larry began. He thought he should correct Attila's mistake. But he was speechless when the horse-head woman ran a finger through her luxurious mane. She gave a toothy grin to Attila. The Hun warlord rolled his eyes and blushed.

Dexter chattered as he held up a broken nose to a centaur. This particular statue already looked mismatched. He represented the mythical creature that had the torso of a man attached to the body of a horse. This particular statue was complete except for a missing nose. The centaur clopped forward and reached down toward the monkey. Dexter grinned mischievously and backed away from the centaur's reach.

"Dex..." warned Larry.

The monkey didn't heed Larry's warning. Instead, Dexter held the nose over his head and chattered his little monkey laugh. The noseless centaur scowled and pounded a hoof against the marble floor. Dexter spun and scampered out of the room. The centaur galloped after him.

"Dex!" yelled Larry as he gave chase.

He followed the centaur into a long chamber. A sign across the entrance let him know that he had entered the Hall of the Hunt. Its paneled walls were lined with taxidermy animal heads mounted on wooden plaques. There were exotic animals from all over the world—wild boars, rhinoceroses, bighorn sheep. The tablet had worked its magic with stuffed creatures, as well. The animal heads turned to watch Larry run by.

Larry slid to a stop beside the large centaur. The creature snorted as he glared up at an ornate chandelier suspended from the high ceiling. It swung lazily as Dexter dangled from it.

Larry put his hands on his hips and glared up at the monkey. "Dex, give the horse guy his nose."

Dexter grinned once more and then tossed the marble nose down at the mythical creature. The centaur caught it with one hand and fit it to his face. Now complete, the centaur snorted once more before clopping back toward the Greek gallery.

The mounted heads turned to watch him leave. Then they tracked the movements of the rest of Larry's friends as they entered.

Larry pointed up at the monkey. "Dex, if you pull something like that again…" began Larry. He finished his threat by pointing to the animal heads around him. Dexter seemed to get the idea. He hopped down and scampered over to the rest of the group.

Suddenly, the ground shook. The chandeliers jingled and the mounted animal heads rattled on the walls. The immense vibrations were rhythmic, as if they were made by footsteps—the footsteps of something with massive feet. The sound grew louder. Then the source of the sound turned a corner and came into view.

A giant dinosaur skeleton tromped into the other end of the long room. It lumbered on four bony feet and swung a skeletal tail. Two horns jutted from the fossilized frill encircling the top of its skull. Just in front of its hollow eyes, another horn protruded from its bony snout. It was the fossilized skeleton of a massive triceratops.

"Lawrence, I think it's safe to say we're in trouble," said Teddy. He crept closer to Larry as the dinosaur tromped forward.

"We'll just be down here if anyone needs us," said Octavius. He and Jedediah ducked behind the fur cuff of Attila's hat.

At first, Larry was startled by the approaching living fossil. But then he spotted something hooked on the wall among the mounted animal heads. "I know how to deal with this guy," he told Teddy.

Larry moved to the wall and hefted a large elephant tusk from an ornate plaque. Holding the heavy ivory shaft in both hands, he stepped forward to meet the oncoming dinosaur.

"Dad, what are you doing?" asked Nick.

Larry shot a smile over his shoulder. "How do you think I tamed your pal, Rexy?" he asked.

When Larry first became the night guard at the Museum of Natural History, the first creature he saw come to life was Rexy—the terrifying skeleton of a Tyrannosaurus Rex. At first Larry didn't know what to do. Luckily, Cecil, his predecessor as night guard, had left a specific list of instructions. Number one on that list: throw the bone. Larry soon realized that Rexy was more like a giant dog. Only, he was a giant dog who enjoyed playing fetch with one of his own rib bones.

Larry held up the tusk as he approached the triceratops. "Hey big fella," he said in a gentle voice. He wiggled the tusk in the air. "Want to play fetch?"

The dinosaur skeleton stopped and trained its hollow eye sockets on the tusk. Its horned head tracked the tusk as Larry moved it from side to side.

"Yeah, it's gonna be fun," Larry continued. Larry raised the tusk over his head. "You ready?" He leaned back and hurled the tusk over the dinosaur's head. "Go get it!"

The skeleton turned its skull to watch the tusk sail down the long hall. The ivory shaft clattered to the ground, spinning as it slid along the floor. Once the tusk came to a stop, the triceratops turned its head back to Larry.

"Go get it." Larry waved it away with his hands.

The dinosaur cocked its head, as if trying to understand.

"All you," continued Larry. "Go on."

The fossilized skeleton squared its head and opened its mouth wide.

ROOOOOOOOOOAAAAAAAAR!

"Huh," said Nick. "Not a big fetcher."

"Lawrence, may I suggest a different plan?" asked Teddy.

Larry slowly backed away from the dinosaur. "What's that?"

Teddy took in a deep breath. "Run!!!"

CHAPTER 4

Larry and the others sprinted through the Hall of the Hunt as the giant skeleton galloped after them. The mounted animal heads turned in unison, watching the frenzied parade. The group exited the hall and took a sharp right down another corridor. The lumbering beast couldn't make the turn as easily. The skeleton smashed into a glass case against the wall. Ancient tools and artifacts scattered everywhere. The collision bought them some time, but not much.

"I thought a triceratops was a plant eater!" said Nick.

"He doesn't want to eat us," said Ahkmenrah. "He just wants to kill us!"

Larry spotted the entrance to another exhibit. Over the entranceway a large sign announced the History and Myth of the Middle Ages exhibit. Beyond lay a large gallery full of tapestries, armor, and medieval weaponry. Larry didn't care about the exhibit itself. What appealed to him were the two large wooden doors on either side of the entrance.

"Follow me!" he ordered.

Everyone darted through the entrance. Once his friends were inside, Larry swung the massive doors shut behind him. He snatched a large battle axe from the wall and pushed its long shaft through the door handles, barring the doors.

Larry caught his breath. "I think we're good."

Suddenly, the doors erupted in a mass of wood chips and splinters as the triceratops smashed through. The group scattered back as the dinosaur skeleton shoved its way inside. The great beast lunged at them and swung its head to one side. One of his horns hooked a strap on Nick's backpack.

"Nick!" shouted Larry.

The creature shook its head and Nick flew across the room. The backpack ripped open and the gold tablet flew out. It spun across the floor as Nick tumbled in the other direction.

"I'm okay!" said Nick. He got to his feet and scrambled in the tablet's direction.

"Get back!" Larry ordered.

"I got it!" Nick didn't listen. He had only made it a couple of steps before the dinosaur looked his way. Nick froze.

"Get back!" repeated Larry. "I'm serious!"

Nick slowly backed away as the skeletal beast lowered its head. It was ready to charge. It was ready to attack Larry's son.

Acting quickly, Larry stepped forward and waved his arms above his head. "Hey, buddy! Over here! You and me!"

The triceratops turned its head toward Larry and snorted. Larry kept waving until the dinosaur turned its entire body to face him. Larry inched over to a nearby display and hefted a mace off the wall. The medieval weapon had a long wooden handle with a studded iron ball on one end.

"You don't want to fetch?" asked Larry, brandishing the heavy weapon with both hands. "Fetch on this!"

"What does that even mean?" asked Nick.

The giant skeleton growled as it lumbered over to Larry. The night guard swung the mace in front of him, trying to keep the beast back. With shocking speed, the dinosaur darted its head forward and bit the mace. The wooden handle snapped in half. Larry was left with a short stick while the business end of the weapon fell through the skeleton's open jawbones. The spiked ball clattered to the floor.

Before Larry could think of what to do next, the triceratops pushed forward. It pinned Larry against a suit of armor against a wall. The horn on the skeleton's snout was inches from Larry's face as the creature snapped at him. The dinosaur's two long horns dug into the wall on either side of the armor. Luckily, the horns were just long enough to keep the beast from being able to bite Larry. Frustrated, the triceratops let out another terrifying roar.

ROOOOOOOOOOAAAAAAR!

"Need some help, friend?" asked a muffled voice behind him.

Larry squirmed to look over his shoulder. The voice sounded as if it came from the suit of armor.

"Duck!" ordered the voice.

Larry did as he was told, and the suit of armor sprung into action. The knight raised his right arm, bringing up a gleaming broadsword. The heavy blade slammed against the triceratops' snout. The dinosaur staggered back, stunned.

Larry took the opening and leaped from between the knight and dinosaur. As soon as he was clear, the knight stepped forward, raising his sword for another blow. This time, the triceratops was ready. It cocked its head and parried the blow with one of its long horns. This didn't deter the knight. The sparkling suit of armor spun around and whipped his shining blade at the beast. The skeleton blocked this blow as well, but it took a step back from its new opponent.

Larry joined Nick and the others as they watched the amazing duel. As big as the dinosaur was, the knight was fearless. His sword was a blur as he easily deflected blows from the creature's horns and snapping jaws. The behemoth jerked his head as it stabbed and slashed at its armored foe.

The dinosaur growled in frustration as it took several steps back. One of its clawed feet pawed at the ground as it lowered its head. It was about to charge. As soon as the beast lumbered forward, the knight charged as well. Then, just before the two were going to collide, the armored figure dropped to his knees and leaned back. He skidded along the floor, beneath the dinosaur. The knight slashed at the skeleton's front legs, knocking them out from under it. The creature grunted as it slid, head first, toward Larry and the others. It stopped just inches short of them, and the knight got to his feet behind it.

The ground shook as the triceratops clambered to its feet. It spun to face the knight and its long bony tail came around.

"Look out!" warned Larry.

Everyone was fast enough to duck under the tail—everyone but Attila. The bones slammed into his chest and sent him flying across the room.

As the knight and dinosaur continued their battle, Larry ran over to Attila. The Hun was stunned but okay. Being a warlord, Attila could take such a powerful blow. Being a wax mannequin, even better.

Larry was about to help Attila to his feet when the dinosaur swung around again. This time, Attila escaped in time, lying back down as the bones came around. Larry sprang up and the tail passed between himself and Attila. They both grunted as Larry came down hard on the Hun. Larry glanced over his shoulder to see the tail rise high into the air. He and Attila screamed in unison as it swung back toward them. Gripping each other in a bear hug, the two rolled away just as the bony tail slammed against the ground.

Larry and Attila scrambled to their feet as the knight and dinosaur continued to battle. Then the brave knight did something quite uncharacteristic of a brave knight; he ran away. He sprinted across the large room with the triceratops galloping after him. Larry frowned, glancing at Attila. The Hun warlord shrugged his shoulders.

The armored knight headed straight for an exit at the other end of the gallery. Then, at the last minute, he veered to the left and ran toward a large marble column. Not slowing down, he ran up the pillar, pushed off, and spun around in midair. He slid down the dinosaur's bony back just before the beast crashed into the pillar. The knight twirled his sword as he casually strode back toward Larry and the others.

"Now things get interesting," said the knight.

Behind him, the dinosaur wobbled on its feet. It shook its head and glanced around, looking for its foe. It spotted the knight and spun its bony body around. The beast lowered its head and charged at the knight.

Larry pointed over the knight's shoulder. "Uh, you may want to...turn around."

When the knight reached Larry, he handed over his sword. "Hold this, would you?"

Larry took the broadsword's handle and the heavy blade clanged against the floor. The knight chuckled and turned at the last minute to face the dinosaur. The armored man reared back and punched the beast square on the snout. The enormous skeleton slammed to a stop as if hitting a brick wall. It let out a whimper before whirling around and running away.

"Okay, that was actually very cool," said Nick.

The knight stepped over to the golden tablet on the floor. He snatched it up, examined it, and walked it back to Larry. He handed it over.

"Thanks," said Larry, taking the tablet. He handed the knight his sword. "That was...amazing."

The knight sheathed his sword and unbuckled the side of his helmet. He slowly pulled it off his head. Silken blonde locks of hair fluttered free. The man had gleaming blue eyes and wore a neatly trimmed beard. "Sir Lancelot," he said. "At your service."

"*The* Sir Lancelot?" Teddy's eyes widened. "Of Camelot?"

Lancelot flashed a gleaming white smile. "Is there another?"

"I read about you as boy," said Teddy. His own wide grin appeared. "Lancelot, King Arthur, Guinevere, the Knights of the Round Table!"

Larry stared at Teddy. He had never seen the man so starstruck before.

Teddy beamed. "Everything I know about bravery, honor, and chivalry, I learned from you."

The knight gave a small bow. "You're welcome."

Teddy rushed forward to shake the knight's hand. "Theodore Roosevelt. President of the United States of America."

"Ahkmenrah. Fourth King of the Four Kings," said the pharaoh. "We are in your debt."

Attila stepped forward and pounded his chest with one fist. "Attila. Dahkmor harash."

Lancelot grinned at the Hun but shook his head. "I have no idea what that means."

Sacajawea stepped forward. "I am Sacajawea."

The knight gave a deep bow, then gently took one of Sacajawea's hands. "These are perilous lands. This is no place for the fairer sex."

Sacajawea raised an eyebrow. "Excuse me?"

Lancelot gestured at his surroundings. "A woman is far too delicate for such an adventure."

70

Sacajawea jerked her hand from his grasp. "When I walked three thousand miles through uncharted wilderness, in moccasins, with a baby strapped to my back...we ran out of food and had to eat candles." She nodded. "I think I'll be okay."

Lancelot chuckled. "Worry not, my lady." He gestured to the others. "There are brave men here to protect you."

Sacajawea rolled her eyes. "Lucky me." She was about to say more but Teddy took her hand and smiled nervously.

Dexter marched up to the knight and chirped. "That's Dexter," said Larry.

The knight bent low to see the monkey. As the man's face drew close, Dexter raised a little monkey hand, ready to slap.

"Dex," warned Larry. "Good behavior!"

Instead of slapping the knight's face (the monkey's usual way of making a first impression), Dexter lowered his paw and gave a deep bow. He ended it with an elaborate flourish of his other paw. Lancelot chuckled and stood upright.

"Okay," said Larry with a frown. He wasn't expecting the monkey to act civilized for a change. He shook his head and looked back at the knight. "I'm Larry, and this is my son, Nick."

Lancelot gave Nick a curt bow. "You have a noble face, Nick."

"Oh...thanks," said Nick.

Lancelot studied Larry's face and pointed at him. "And you...you remind me of a man I knew at Camelot."

"Oh yeah?" Larry smiled. "One of the... Knights of the Round Table?"

Lancelot shook his head. "Erik. Our fool."

Larry frowned.

Lancelot's smile widened and he addressed the others. "The funniest fool I ever met. He was so good that he didn't even have to say anything. He'd just walk into the room and you'd begin to laugh."

The knight turned back to Larry, examined his face some more, and then burst into laughter. Larry shook his head.

"You have what he had," said the Knight between guffaws. "The gift! You could be a fool. If you get one of those funny little hats. You know? With the bells?"

Larry sighed and nodded. "Yes."

Lancelot's eyes widened. "Yes," he repeated and roared with laughter once more. He glanced at the others. "Did I tell you? He has the gift!" He doubled over and bellowed then took a deep breath. "He does what seems like nothing. A deadpan, expressionless reaction. Limp-faced almost." He pointed to Larry's deadpan, expressionless reaction. "And yet it's funny! Just like Erik!"

Larry nodded. "Thank you. Okay."

Lancelot snorted with laughter and waved for Larry to stop. The knight pulled a long silk scarf from the cuff of one gauntlet and blotted the tears from his eyes. The scarf was decorated with beautiful embroidery. Stitched on the scarf was the image of a mighty castle surrounded by peaceful woodlands.

Lancelot held up the design. "Ah, Camelot!" He turned to the others. "I left it long ago. And someday, I shall return. To its mighty towers. To King Arthur and Queen Guinevere." He sniffed the scarf. "Sweet, kind, fair, and beauteous Guinevere."

Teddy leaned forward and whispered into Larry's ear. "Lancelot was the subject of many legends, but one thread runs through them all . . . he was deeply in love with King Arthur's wife, Guinevere."

Larry frowned. "Why are you telling me this?"

Teddy shrugged. "I assumed you might be unfamiliar with this information."

Larry opened his mouth to tell him that everybody was familiar with that information. He stopped himself and patted Teddy on the shoulder. "You were right. Thank you."

Lancelot stuffed the scarf back into his gauntlet. "But I am sworn not to return until I have completed my quest." He struck a noble pose and raised one finger high above his head. "I must find...the Holy Grail!"

Larry glanced at the others then back at Lancelot. "Well, good luck with that." He gave the knight a wave. "Thank you very much for the assist. That was impressive. We're just trying to get to Egypt." He pointed to the doorway. "So...that way?"

Lancelot's eyes widened. "I will lead you!"

Larry held up a hand. "No, no. It's okay"

Lancelot unsheathed his sword and gave it a twirl. "There is a strange magic in the air and dangerous beasts are afoot. I follow the code of *chivalry*. The duty of a true knight is to protect and care for those in need." He marched toward the exit. "We're off!"

"I guess he's coming with us," said Larry. "Okay, cool. Nick, Teddy, Dex..." he glanced around. "Where are Jed and Octavius?"

Everyone began scanning the floor. Attila patted the fur brim of his hat. He frowned. "Bor doshala!"

They were gone.

CHAPTER 5

L arry led the way as they backtracked to the
Hall of the Hunt. The museum was huge and
his miniature friends were...miniature. He
worried that they wouldn't be able to spot them in
this strange new environment.

"They must have fallen out when we were
running," said Teddy.

"Octavius!" called Ahkmenrah.

"Jedediah!" called Teddy.

Sacajawea knelt and examined the debris strewn
across the floor. An expert tracker, she quickly
picked up their trail. "Ah! They fell and rolled this
way." She leaned closer. "Then...they vanished." She
glanced around until her eyes fell upon a rectangular
heating vent on the floor. Larry knelt beside her
and examined the vent. Its long blades were just far
apart enough for the little miniatures to fit through.
To confirm this, Sacajawea reached down and
plucked a tiny piece of red fabric snagged on one

of the blades. She held it up to Larry. It was Octavius' cape.

Larry leaned toward the vent. "Jed! Octavius!" There was no reply.

"They won't last long in those heating vents, Lawrence," said Teddy.

Larry hopped up and scanned the area. He spotted what he was looking for and ran over to the wall. He punched a few buttons on the heating control panel. "And…shutting down." The soft hum of the museum's heating system faded to silence.

Attila crouched down and put his face next to the vent. "Koolaskadiah! Bchactavious!" He turned his head to listen for a response. He waited for a moment and then shook his head. "Moskasheeloo."

Larry joined Attila beside the vent. He pulled off the bladed cover. "Okay. They could be anywhere between here and the intake vent." He turned to the capuchin. "Dex, you're going in."

The little monkey chattered angrily and shook his head.

Larry sighed. "Listen to me, Dexter. I know we haven't always seen eye to eye. We've had our tussles. But this is bigger than us." He pointed to the open vent. "Those little guys are out there. They're alone, they're scared, and they're cold."

"They're in a *heating* vent, Dad," said Nick.

Larry shot a frustrated look up at Nick. Then he turned back to Dexter. "Even worse. They're alone, scared...and hot."

Dexter lowered his head.

Larry put a hand on the monkey's shoulder. "Come on, buddy. You're their best shot."

Dexter gave a nervous smile and nodded his head.

"Great," said Larry. He reached a hand up to Nick. "I need your phone. For Dex."

Nick raised an eyebrow. "Okay...why not *your* phone?"

"Nick," said Larry.

Lancelot shook his head. "I don't understand one thing that is going on here."

"Neither do I," agreed Nick. He reluctantly dug into his pocket.

Teddy leaned in. "Lawrence, Dexter's a clever monkey, but I don't think he can make a phone call."

Larry shook his head. "He doesn't need to. I'm set up to track Nick's phone."

Nick examined his phone. "Wait, what? You track my phone?"

"Yeah, Nick," Larry replied. "I'm your dad, I'm looking out for you."

Nick glowered at him. "Spying on someone is not the same thing as looking out for someone."

"I was worried about you," explained Larry. "Worried about you...socially."

"Why?" asked Nick.

Larry nodded. "Every night I'd check up on you. You never went anywhere." Larry rolled his eyes. "Obviously it makes a lot more sense now."

Nick thrust out the phone. "Wow. Okay, here ...keep it. I don't want it anymore."

Larry took the phone and moved to a shattered display case. He pulled a couple of strips of fabric from the display and tied them around the phone. He crouched beside Dexter and glanced back up at Nick. "Any last-minute texts you want to send? iChat? gChat? snapChat?"

Nick crossed his arms. "No, I'm good."

"Okay, because it's going on the monkey's back," said Larry. He tied the phone around Dexter's shoulders. When Larry was done, Dexter wore the phone like a tiny backpack.

"All right, Dex," said Larry. "Bring them home, buddy. Down the hole."

Dexter gave Larry a quick salute and then hopped into the open vent. The monkey crawled out of sight. A faint *hi-yah!* echoed through the vent as Nick's phone received a text message.

Larry fished out his phone from his pocket and pulled up the tracking app. At once, his screen displayed a tiny blue dot, representing Nick's phone. The dot moved slowly away from the center of the screen.

Larry led the way as he followed the direction of the dot on his screen. The others stayed close while Nick grumpily brought up the rear.

Sacajawea fell into step beside Larry. "The great Shoshone trackers learned to think like the animal," she said. "So they could know where it went even when they lost its trail."

Larry nodded at the phone. "Yeah, also the blue dot thing helps."

Sacajawea glanced back at Nick. "It's a difficult age. But it's good that he's here. A journey teaches many things. I'll never regret having my son with me on my travels."

Larry glanced up. "Yeah? You think he learned something?"

"Of course not, he was a baby," replied Sacajawea. Then she smiled at him "But *I* learned a great deal."

The group moved down the corridor, passing the entrances to many amazing exhibits. Larry paid them little mind. Instead, his attention stayed focused on the tiny blue dot that represented Nick's phone. As the group came to an intersection of four corridors, Larry studied the phone to see in which direction the blue dot moved.

"Okay, take a right here," said Larry.

A burst of laughter erupted behind him. "Take a right here," repeated Lancelot. He chuckled. "The gift of laughter. Thank you, my friend."

Larry turned back and glared at Lancelot. "I said, *'take a right here.'*"

Lancelot grinned and nodded. "It was the *way* you said it."

Larry shook his head and went back to tracking Dexter. They followed the blue dot until it led them through a large archway and into a giant atrium. Larry lost focus on the phone as he took in the amazing sight before him. The enormous space was filled with newly awakened exhibits from all over the world. Japanese bronze heron statures soared above them. They glided just under the high glass ceiling. A stone lion licked its paw and wiped its head. It looked like a giant kitten giving itself a bath. Two huge, Assyrian lamassu tussled in the corner. The lamassu were mythical creatures with lion bodies, wings, and human heads with long beards. The strange animals wrestled like puppies as they pounced on each other and rolled across the floor. An armored horse trotted by in one direction while Persian peacock sculptures strutted by, glittering with gemstones.

Larry's eyes darted back to the blue dot on his phone. He led them across the atrium, following Dexter's trail.

Lancelot strode next to Larry. "First quest?" asked the knight.

"Not exactly," said Larry.

"Do you always put the monkey in charge?" asked Lancelot.

Larry shook his head. "He's not in charge, we're just following him."

"That's what being in charge means," Lancelot explained. "I thought you were going to Egypt."

Larry frowned. "We are. But we have to do this first."

Lancelot chuckled. "That's not the way a quest works, my friend. A quest is only one thing. It's not ... find the Holy Grail and a monkey."

"Yeah, well ... my guys are missing and Dexter's going to find them," said Larry.

"How long have you known them?" asked Lancelot. "The missing ones. The little trolls?"

Larry scowled. "They're not trolls. They're miniatures. They're my friends."

"Friends fall by the wayside," said Lancelot. "The weak perish. Happens on every quest. That's why you have armies instead of just ... two people."

"Look, the reason I'm going to Egypt is to save my friends," said Larry. "So it's not two things. It's the same thing."

"So, what's the quest?" asked Lancelot. He rubbed his hands together. "Gold? Flaming sword? Fountain of Youth?"

"Magic tablet," replied Larry.

"Hmm," Lancelot nodded knowingly. "And where is this magic tablet you seek? Does it reside in the great and vast unknown beyond hope and dream?"

"Nope. Right there." Larry jutted a thumb over his shoulder. "That thing Ahk is holding."

Lancelot leaned closer. "Shouldn't be hard to take it from him," the knight whispered. "He seems well toned and lean, but weak."

"No, I'm not trying to get it. I'm trying to fix it," Larry explained. "Something's wrong with it." He shook his head. "You know what? It's really kind of complicated."

Lancelot shrugged. "It might be less complicated if you stop following a chimpanzee."

"He's not a chimpanzee," said Larry. "He's a capuchin." The blue dot stopped on the screen and Larry stopped, as well. The others filed passed him gazing at all the living exhibits around them. Lancelot moved to Teddy.

"The fool seems agitated," murmured Lancelot.

Larry shook his head in disgust but kept an eye on the blue dot.

"That's often his way," Teddy replied. "But he's no fool, I assure you. Lawrence has been our leader and guardian for many years now."

"Is it true what he says?" the knight asked Ahkmenrah. "The tablet you carry is magic?"

"It is indeed," replied the young pharaoh. He pointed at their surroundings. "Everything you see around you has come to life tonight for the very first time. All because of this tablet."

Lancelot ran his gloved fingers over the tablet's tiles. "Amazing." He looked up at the exhibits around them. "Then...they're not real?"

"Once the tablet brings them to life, they're as real as any of us," Teddy explained.

"Yes, but we're real people. They're just...things. And they don't even know?" Lancelot laughed. "How pathetic! They must be unbelievably stupid!"

Teddy gave a sympathetic smile. "It can be confusing at first."

Lancelot waved at a nearby frog statue as it hopped by. "Hello, frog! Keep hopping! You're real!" He stifled a laugh and rolled his eyes.

Ahkmenrah opened his mouth to speak but Teddy took the pharaoh's arm. The former president shook his head ever so slightly. Larry could tell that Teddy didn't think it was the best time to tell Lancelot the entire truth—that the knight also owed his newfound life to the magic of the tablet. Larry agreed. And he sure wouldn't be the one to shatter the knight's fantasy. The news was always better coming from fellow museum exhibits rather than from him. Besides, first things first. They had to focus on tracking Dexter.

Larry turned his attention back to his phone. The dot moved away from the center of the screen in a different direction. Larry looked up, following its path. He saw the entrance of another part of the museum before him.

"Looks like we'll have to cut through Asia," Larry told the others.

He began walking toward the new wing when Lancelot stepped in front of him, blocking his path. The knight drew his sword.

"You should have told me the truth," said Lancelot.

Larry took a step back, bracing himself for battle. But then Lancelot put the tip of his sword to the ground and knelt before it.

"A fool gives birth to a hero. Wondrous indeed!" He looked up and gazed into Larry's eyes. "You carry a treasure more precious than all the world's gold. My soul, my heart, and my steel are at your command until your quest is complete. I shall not leave your side until you have safely arrived in Egypt." He bowed his head.

Larry glanced around at the others. Teddy shrugged.

Larry tentatively patted the knight on the head. "Okay." Lancelot grasped Larry's hand and pressed it to his lips for a long kiss. *This isn't weird at all,* thought Larry.

Octavius peered over the edge of a deep shaft on the ductwork floor. He and Jedediah had been traveling for what seemed like miles to their tiny legs. They hadn't found a way out of the heating system until now. Unfortunately, the only way out seemed to be a dark shaft leading straight down. It was an endless pit that disappeared into utter darkness.

When they had originally fallen through the first vent, the two miniatures were blown through the ducts in a whirlwind. They had been stuck on a lint-covered air filter until the wind inexplicably stopped. The miniatures had tried to retrace their steps but they heard the monstrous footsteps of something in the ductworks with them. They had run from the unseen beast hoping to stay away from whatever danger it possessed.

Jed leaned over to gaze into the dark vent with Octavius. "Can't see much. We could jump down and hope for the best."

Octavius frowned. "We have no idea what's down there."

Just then, the echoing footsteps returned. The entire metal tunnel vibrated beneath their feet as the creature drew near.

"No idea what's up here either," said Jedediah.

The footfalls sounded like thunder. They turned to see a dark shape round a corner several feet away. Then the creature gave the most peculiar roar.

Hi-yah!

"Aaaaghhh!" screamed Jedediah and Octavius. Without another word between them, they leaped into the shadowy pit before them.

They fell for a long time in total darkness. Then light grew around them as they rapidly approached another slatted vent cover. Both the tiny cowboy and miniature Roman commander slipped between the blades and were suddenly bathed in bright light. Octavius squinted, trying to get a bearing on their whereabouts. Before he could make out anything, they landed on something hard. They tumbled to the ground.

As they got to their feet, Octavius' eyes slowly adjusted to the light. He took in their new surroundings. They had landed on a normal-sized brick street. It was a normal size for them, anyway. Stone buildings lined the road and large structures spread out as far as the eye could see. Unbelievably,

Jed and Octavius stood in the center of a deserted city—a city that was just the right size.

Octavius recognized the architecture at once. "This is a Roman city," he said. "I can feel the familiar pull of history in its very foundation."

Jed tilted back his cowboy hat and glanced around. "Where the heck is everybody?"

The two walked along the empty streets. They peeked in doorways and looked through windows, but there wasn't another soul about. The place was utterly deserted.

Octavius furrowed his brow. "This town looks familiar," he said. "I could swear I've seen it before."

The street ended at a barrier of thick glass. It turned out that they stood inside a miniature display. It was similar to the ones in the diorama room in their museum back in New York.

Octavius put his hands on the glass and looked down. The display was labeled with a small plaque below. Perhaps he could find out where they were. The writing was upside down and difficult to read. "Iiepmop," read Octavius. He thought for a moment. "Hmm...doesn't ring a bell."

On the other side of the glass, near their display, a large marble bust sat atop a stone pillar. The sculpture was the head and shoulders of an ancient Roman man. He stared at them with wide eyes.

The man moved his mouth, speaking to them, but Octavius couldn't hear through the thick glass.

"What's that, citizen?" Octavius asked. "I'm having trouble hearing you."

The bust repeated what it had said but they still couldn't make out the muffled words.

"Still not understanding ya, pally!" said Jedediah.

The bust opened his mouth wide as he spoke, as if he were shouting. He seemed to be repeating one word over and over again.

Jed pointed to the gallery floor. "Hey, look!" Several Roman miniatures ran across the room, away from the Roman city display. They screamed and pointed back to the empty city. "Why are they stampedin' like that?"

Octavius banged on the glass and shouted at them. "Hello! What are you doing? Come back to Iiepmop!" He spread his arms wide. "There's plenty of room!"

Jed scratched his head and looked at the plaque below. "Iiepmop...are you sure you read that right, amigo?"

Octavius checked the plaque again and realized that he had made a mistake. Just as it came to him that he had read the name backwards, the ground shook beneath their feet. Octavius and Jedediah tried to stay balanced as they slowly turned to see the giant mountain on the other side of the city. The top of the mountain exploded and streams of red hot lava poured down its sides. The molten rock began to fill the city itself.

"Oh. Right…" said Octavius.

The name of the volcano was Mount Vesuvius. The city that it destroyed in ancient times was called Pompeii. It was the name the bust across the gallery had been repeating. It was the name of the doomed city in which Jed and Octavius stood at that very moment.

Larry led the group into the Asia wing of the museum. The walls were lined with beautiful Chinese scroll paintings. Because of the magic tablet, each of them was alive with activity. Ornately painted waves crashed upon picturesque shores. Goldfish with flowing fins swam through crystal-clear ponds. Brightly feathered birds whistled from snowy treetops. The group spread out to take in the magical sights around them. Teddy took Sacajawea's hand. They smiled at each other as they strolled through their beautiful surroundings.

Up ahead, Lancelot pointed to Nick's arm. "I see you have the name of a lady on your arm. Along with a mysterious series of numbers."

Nick laughed and rubbed his arm. "Andrea, yeah."

"Are those Druidic cryptograms?" asked the knight.

Nick shook his head. "Nope. It's basically just her cell number."

Lancelot grinned. "Ah, so this Lady Andrea is your Guinevere." He pulled the embroidered scarf from his gauntlet. "My lady gave me a favor as well. On Joust Day." He held the silk scarf to his nose, closed his eyes, and breathed deeply. He opened his eyes and smiled. "Arthur was not pleased." He leaned close to Nick. "That's the real reason he sent me in search of the Grail. He hoped I'd never return." He straightened. "And I am bound not to. Not until I find it."

The knight tucked the scarf back into his metal glove. "Does anyone stand between you and your lady love?"

Nick glanced back at his father. Larry pretended to study his phone and not to be eavesdropping on his son. Of course, he had just admitted to tracking his son's phone. At this point, what could a little eavesdropping hurt?

"Yeah, no …" Nick began. "I mean … my dad kind of messed things up when he came home early the other night."

Lancelot held up a finger. "Let no man stand between you and your destiny."

"Destiny might be overstating it," replied Nick. "I mean…we just have calculus together. But yeah…I hear you."

Larry frowned. He wasn't sure the mythical knight was such a good role model for Nick.

When the group reached the other side of the gallery, they came across several Buddha sculptures. Many of the peaceful statues sat on carved cushions, their eyes shut, in deep meditation. Other Buddha sculptures smiled and waved at the group. A particularly large Buddha, near the exit, put a finger to his lips and shushed the new arrivals.

Larry heeded the warning and stopped. The Buddha kept his finger to his lips while he pointed at the open doorway. Larry didn't know what he was indicating and was about to step through when a tiny golden creature stepped out from behind the Buddha's display. The living figurine had the torso of a man with the head and legs of a bird. Its tiny talons clicked on the marble floor as it scurried forward.

"Oh. Hey, little guy," said Larry. "Just passing through."

"It's Garuda from Tibet," explained Teddy. "A charming fellow, representative of wisdom as well as a protector from mythical serpents. I had to carry one of them down Mt. Kailash after I lost a wager with a monk."

Larry started walking again but the Garuda statue moved forward, blocking his path. Larry stepped to the left and the statue did the same. Larry sidestepped to the right and the Garuda blocked his way again.

"You know what? Fun game," said Larry. "But I don't have time right now."

The Garuda shrugged its feathered shoulders and stepped aside to let them pass. The group cautiously moved through the doorway. They rounded a corner and spotted what the tiny protector was trying to protect them from.

A humongous bronze snake was coiled in the center of the gallery. Its snout was barely visible and its eyes were closed. Its giant body slowly inflated and deflated as it snored loudly.

Lancelot's face lit up. "A dragon!"

Larry pulled everyone back behind a large pillar. He craned his neck as he peeked out to read the plaque beside the sleeping beast.

"It's not a dragon," Larry whispered. "It's…Xiangliu. A mythical snake demon."

"Well, it looks like a dragon," said Lancelot. "I say we kill it."

"It's asleep," said Larry.

The knight thought a moment. "Right. Not very sporting to kill it in its sleep." He snapped his fingers.

Just four historical figures, a monkey, and a night guard riding a bus.
Perfectly normal, right?

"Guinevere! I'm coming, my love!"

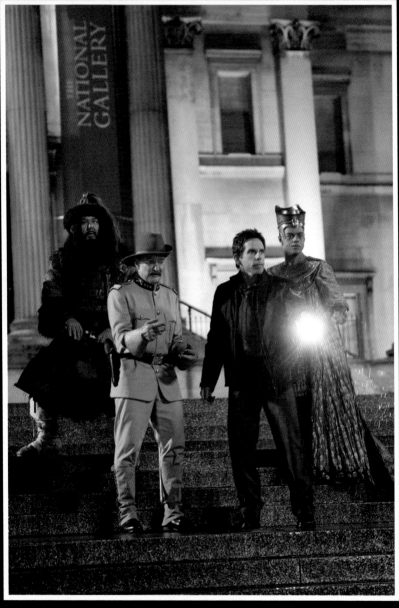

"Lawrence, I can't move my arms. I fear we're becoming less useful by the minute."

"Lancelot came this way...traveling half an acre per hour."

"Nicky, you're my son. You're always going to be my problem."

Triceratops. Little known fact: not big on playing *fetch*.

"You won't get away with

Laa the Neanderthal makes a new friend *and* gets a makeover.

The planetarium's grand re-opening didn't go quite as planned.

Dexter steals a centaur's nose—just another night at the museum.

Every boy must slay his own dr⸻⸻⸻time. Not a fan of snakes, Larry

"By the beard of Jupiter, there is no escape!"

Larry Daley gets some unexpected help for his mission to the British Museum.

"The tablet is losing its power. I warned them not to move it. I specifically said *the end will come*. How hard is that to understand?"

"Let's wake it up, and *then* kill it." He put a hand on his sword. "I will go first and I shall take the boy."

Larry shook his head. "No, you're not taking the boy."

"Why not?" asked Lancelot.

"Because he's ... a boy," replied Larry. "And we don't need to kill it."

"Do you want him to stay a boy forever?" asked Lancelot. He gave a thoughtful look. "Larry, there comes a time when everyone must slay his own dragon."

"That's a figure of speech," said Larry.

Lancelot grinned. "Not where I come from."

Larry waved his arms. "We're not slaying anything. We're going around." He held up his phone. "We have to go now or we might lose the signal. Now shush!"

Slowly and quietly, the group crept out from behind the pillar. They moved around the sleeping demon, only stopping when the beast snorted and twitched in its sleep. Once it had settled down again, the group inched by. They were almost clear when an emerald light shined into Larry's eyes. He glanced back and saw that the tablet was glowing green again.

"No, no, no ..." whispered Larry.

Teddy's eyes went wide and he shot a finger into the air. "Ask not what your country can do for you!"

He said in a perfect, but very loud, John F. Kennedy voice. "Ask what *you* can do for your country!"

"Teddy!" said Larry.

He moved back to quiet Teddy but stopped at Sacajawea. She stared straight ahead. She was stone-faced, as if in a trance. Larry waved his hands in front of her face.

"Sac, you there?" he asked.

Before he could investigate further, a piercing scream erupted from Attila. The once-fierce Hun warlord cowered and pointed just over Larry's shoulder. Larry turned to see the Xiangliu fully awake and coiled, ready to strike. And as if that weren't bad enough, the snake demon turned out to have not one but *nine* fierce heads.

CHAPTER 6

Larry craned his neck up at the towering bronze demon. "That's a lot of heads." Each terrifying head hissed and bared two long fangs.

Lancelot pointed at the demon and smiled at Larry. "There. Now we can kill it!" He drew his sword. "Come on, there's enough heads for all of us! Four and a half each, if it's just me and the boy." He turned to Larry's son. "Have you ever used a blade?"

"Only in World of Warcraft," Nick replied.

Lancelot grinned and pulled a dagger from his belt. He tossed it to Nick who barely caught it by the handle.

"Nick, stay back!" warned Larry.

"Come!" said Lancelot. He rushed toward the demon. He swung his long blade at the striking heads.

"Whoah!" Nick winced and moved back as one of the heads snapped at him.

Lancelot spun around and brought his blade down at the head striking at Nick. The sword bounced off the bronze serpent's neck with a loud *CLANG!*

"Ha!" Lancelot beamed. "I love a challenge!"

Larry felt something wrap around his leg. He was sure it was one of the snake heads. But when he looked down, he saw that it was only Attila. The warlord was curled up in terror as his arms squeezed Larry's leg tightly.

"Attila, what's going on with you, man?" asked Larry. "Get it together."

Larry pried himself away from the Hun just as one of the heads zipped his way. He leaped aside and noticed all of his other friends were out of action. The malfunctioning tablet affected each of them differently. Sacajawea was still frozen in place, Ahkmenrah shuffled around, muttering to himself, and Teddy continued to channel other United States presidents.

"The only thing we have to fear is fear itself!" Teddy shouted in a Franklin Delano Roosevelt voice.

Larry kicked his flashlight out of its holster and caught it in midair. He backhanded a snake head as it came at him. The head continued to attack, but Larry fended away each strike with the butt of his flashlight.

During the battle, Larry chanced a glance at Teddy. The former president was so wrapped up in his other personas that he didn't see one of the demon heads coming at him. Larry struck his own demon head once more before he holstered his light. He ran to Teddy and tackled him to the ground. The serpent's long fangs missed them by inches.

Teddy looked up at Larry and smiled. "Brownie, you're doin' a heckuva job," he said in the voice of George W. Bush.

Jedediah and Octavius raced down the streets of Pompeii. Hot lava flowed behind them as hot ash rained down upon them. Every time they turned down a side street, they met yet another wall of the molten rock. They kept running, but they seemed to be surrounded by lava at every turn.

Jedediah glanced around. "By the beard of Jupiter, there is no escape," the cowboy said in Octavius' voice. "Two noble warriors die this night."

"Last round-up, *kemosabe*," agreed Octavius, speaking in Jed's voice. "Time to slap on the barbecue sauce!"

The two miniatures skid to a stop and stared at each other in confusion.

Jed poked a finger at Octavius' armored chest. The tiny cowboy continued to speak with Octavius' voice. "You sandal-footed serpent! Why have you absconded with my elocution?"

Octavius shrugged. "I ain't got the faintest doggone idea'r."

Lancelot and Nick fought the snake demon back-to-back. Larry wasn't worried about the knight; it was obvious that Lancelot was merely toying with the striking heads. Nick, on the other hand, was fighting for his life. The boy swung the dagger frantically, keeping the attacking heads at bay. Larry had to admit that the young boy was holding his own. Larry was both terrified for his son and proud of him at the same time. Unfortunately, there was no way Lancelot and Nick could hold out forever. They were outnumbered: nine—terrifying demon snake heads, that is—to two.

Larry looked around for anything he could use as a weapon. Occasionally, one of the snake heads would break off from the main battle and strike at the night guard. So far, the best he could do was try to bat it away with a fake torch off the wall. The plastic piece merely bounced off the bronze snake and didn't even phase it.

Luckily, Larry spotted something on the wall he thought he could use—a first-aid station. He ducked under another striking head as he dashed for the wall. He slid to a stop and threw open the panel. He spotted what he'd hoped was inside. Larry pressed a button on the device and snatched up its two paddles. He had found an emergency defibrillator. The apparatus was designed to give a shock to someone undergoing a heart attack. The electric current it produced was usually used to restore a patient's heartbeat to its natural rhythm. Larry hoped it would have a different effect on a bronze snake demon.

An electronic whine filled the air as the machine powered up. With a paddle in each hand, Larry threw himself into the fray. He leaped over one striking head, then ducked under two more. He had to get to the main body. More importantly, he hoped the cables connecting the paddles to the defibrillator would reach. They stretched taut as he slid to a stop beside the giant serpentine demon.

"Clear!" shouted Larry.

He pressed the paddles onto the bronze scales and activated the device. Electricity crackled through Xiangliu's metal body. The snake demon jerked, spasmed, and then froze in place. Larry dropped the paddles and rolled clear as the beast toppled over, clanging to the floor.

"These things really do save lives," said Larry as he held the paddles in the air.

"You deprived us of the death blow!" said Lancelot. He pointed at Larry. "Next time...no sorcery!" He strode over to Nick and put a hand on the boy's shoulder. "You fought bravely. Next time we shall drink dragon's blood from the victor's cup!"

"That was amazing!" said Nick. He handed the dagger back to the knight. "And a little terrifying!"

Lancelot slid the blade back into its sheath. "You are a man now," he said. "From this day forward, you choose your own path. And let no one tell you otherwise."

Larry watched as Nick and Lancelot exchanged a handshake. Maybe the knight was right. Maybe Nick was old enough to choose his own path. Honestly, Larry didn't know what to think. He was still Nick's dad and he still thought it was his job to protect him. A moan from the others caught Larry's attention. He had almost forgotten that there were others that needed his protection, too.

Larry hopped over a lifeless snake head and joined the other members of the group. Attila staggered to his feet. Ahkmenrah shook his head. Sacajawea was moving again. And Teddy was massaging a sore jaw.

"Talk to me, guys," said Larry. "How are you doing?"

Teddy sighed. "It's passed for now."

Ahkmenrah moved aside one of the large snake heads. Underneath was Larry's cell phone. It was smashed.

"How are we going to find them now?" asked Ahkmenrah.

"Uhm, Lawrence?" asked Teddy.

Larry looked over at Teddy. The twenty-sixth president held up a gloved hand. It was frozen stiff, having completely reverted back to its original wax form. Attila reached a hand up to his face. Although he was still alive, his face was rigid and more wax-like, as well.

"I fear we've turned a corner," said Teddy.

Larry looked at the tablet in the pharaoh's hands. The green stain had spread further.

"We're running out of time," said Larry. "We'll have to find Dex and the guys later. We have to get to Egypt now."

"Shouldn't we keep looking for Jed and Octavius?" asked Nick.

"Nick is right," agreed Lancelot. "A true knight never shirks his duties."

Larry sighed. "Thanks for the input, but if we don't get to Egypt soon, we won't be able to save anybody."

Lancelot nodded. "Then this way, my friends."

The group followed the knight out of the Asia wing and into a long corridor. Larry didn't know how close they were to their goal, but he knew they had to get there fast. It was his job to protect his friends and he felt as if he was letting them down. Then again, it was his job to protect someone else, too. Larry fell back to walk with his son.

"Hey, Nick," Larry whispered. "When I tell you to stay back, I mean *stay back*."

Nick rolled his eyes. "Right. Because I'm the boy."

Larry shook his head. "Because I'm your dad. And it's my job to keep you safe. Whether you like it or not."

Nick tightened his lips. Then he opened his mouth ready to reply when Lancelot interrupted him.

"Walk with me, Nicholas," said the knight.

Nick shook his head and walked away from his father. He ran ahead to join Lancelot at the front of the line.

Larry didn't get it. Why couldn't his son realize that everything that Larry did, *everything*, was for his son's own good? He didn't want his son to make the same mistakes that he had made, much less be torn apart by a nine-headed snake demon. What was so difficult to understand? It seemed like the more Larry tried to protect Nick, the further it drove him away. He wondered if all sons felt that way about their fathers.

Larry moved to walk with Ahkmenrah. "Hey, Ahk. When you were growing up, did you and your dad ever butt heads?"

"All the time." Ahkmenrah laughed. "He was a proud man. He never saw me as an equal. Even after I became pharaoh, he never trusted me with the secrets of the tablet."

"How did you work it out?" asked Larry.

Ahkmenrah shrugged. "I had him buried alive with a thousand scorpions."

"What?" asked Larry.

Ahkmenrah grinned. "I'm joking, Larry. A little Egyptian humor." The young pharaoh's smile faded. "No, the truth is...we *didn't* work it out. All these years, I've been arguing with him in my head, trying to sort it out. Thinking about what I'd say to him if I ever got the chance. Guessing what he'd say to me."

"Does that help?" asked Larry.

Ahkmenrah shook his head. "Not really." The pharaoh shrugged. "I honestly don't know how it will be, seeing each other again."

Octavius pressed his back against the wall but there was nowhere else to go. He and Jedediah had run through the streets of Pompeii, always just a few steps in front of the torrent of hot lava. But once they had run into the main square, it was too late. The red-hot liquid slowly made its way toward them from every street, every direction. They were surrounded and had no hope for escape.

At least I'll meet my end on Roman soil, thought Octavius. *Sort of.*

The lava crept closer from all around. Any second, the molten rock would engulf them, turning them to cinders.

Suddenly, there was a loud banging sound above them. The two miniatures looked up to see the heating vent in the ceiling above them. It vibrated as something tried to break through. Then the vent cover flew away and a familiar face appeared. It was Dexter!

The monkey swung down from above and landed atop a tall building. He stood upright and carefully strode across the rooftops. He stopped on the roof above them, taking in the scene. He looked at Jedediah and Octavius and grinned. It was clear the monkey had a plan. Octavius cringed when he realized just what that plan was.

"He wouldn't," said Jedediah.

Octavius closed his eyes. "He must."

Octavius and Jedediah were suddenly drenched in warm liquid. The torrent covered them and the lava mere inches away from their feet. The loud hiss of steam erupted as the molten rock was cooled by the liquid. Octavius opened his eyes to see a wall of black rock surrounding them. The lava had cooled and become solid once more. Dexter had saved them. He had saved them...by peeing on them.

Jedediah wiped his face and grinned up at the monkey. "I'm both disgusted and grateful, you magnificent simian god."

Octavius shook his head. "We shall never speak of what happened here today."

CHAPTER 7

Larry took the lead when he spotted a sign pointing to the Egyptian wing. As leaders went, Lancelot had seemed preoccupied anyway. He and Nick had been talking and laughing the entire trip from Asia.

Larry had hoped that this would be a bonding trip for him and his son. Instead, it was turning out to be a bonding trip for his son and a mythical figure from the Middle Ages. They were now best buddies just because the knight had let Nick wield a dagger and battle some snake demon. It was crazy. And it was reckless, as far as Larry was concerned. He bet that if Lancelot were real *and* had kids, those kids probably wouldn't survive past the age of three... five tops. The knight knew nothing about being a father. Frankly, Larry couldn't wait to get rid of him.

They turned a corner and the large entrance to the Egyptian wing loomed above. A stone arch framed the dark passage beyond.

"This is it," said Larry. He turned and gave Lancelot a wave. "Well, we're here. Lancelot, thanks for all the help. I think we're good."

"Perhaps I should accompany you in," said Lancelot.

"No thanks, we can take it from here." Larry held up his hands. "You have your own quest and everything. The Holy Grail isn't going to find itself."

Lancelot nodded reluctantly then stepped forward. He grasped Larry's arm. "Larry, keeper of the magic tablet, I shall never forget your bravery. Nor your jests." He held up a hand to the others. "Until we meet again, my friends."

Larry nodded. "Goodbye."

Lancelot turned to leave. After taking two steps, he turned and struck a dramatic pose. "I shall not say goodbye. For I know that someday our paths will cross once more. Like threads in the vast and glorious tapestry of life, our destinies are intertwined."

Larry stared at the knight for a moment, making sure he was finished. "Okay, see ya." He turned and led the others through the entrance of the Egyptian wing.

The gallery was dimly lit, with focal lights shining on artifacts in glass cases. Small statues of half-human, half-beast creatures stared at them as they walked by. Slabs of stone were displayed showing Egyptian hieroglyphics come to life. Like the paintings in other parts of the museum, the stone carvings of cats, birds, and ancient Egyptians moved over the stones as if they were a living movie. As Larry and the group moved deeper into the wing, they saw bigger living statues moving about. A large sphinx loped by. A few men with the heads of jackals and cranes milled about. Then things got really creepy. Several sarcophagi lined the passage around them. The ornate coffins stood on end and their lids slowly opened. Ancient mummies shambled out of each of them. The bandaged corpses lumbered toward the group.

Ahkmenrah handed the tablet to Larry. Then the young pharaoh stepped ahead and greeted the mummies. "Friends! Long time!" He shook the dry hand of a nearby mummy. "Imhotep, how are you?" He hugged another. "Ramses!"

Ahkmenrah stopped at a sarcophagus decorated with a painting of a beautiful woman. "It can't be! Is that?" he asked. The lid swung open and a female mummy slowly stepped out. Her bandages weren't as tattered as the rest and they clung tightly to her slender form. Once out of the sarcophagus, she slinked over to the group.

"Larry, meet Cleopatra," said Ahkmenrah. "Luminous beauty of the Fertile Crescent."

"Wow. Cleopatra," said Larry. "Hi."

The woman slowly unwrapped the bandages from her head. She revealed two beautiful brown eyes. Cleopatra had been known for her beauty and now Larry was going to meet her in person. Unfortunately, as she unwound the strips of cloth from the rest of her face, she revealed the usual cracked and withered face of someone who's been dead for thousands of years. Larry tried not to recoil in horror as she leaned forward to kiss him on the cheek.

"Nice...to meet you," said Larry. Her dry lips planted a kiss on one cheek and then moved to the other side of his face. "Okay. Two cheeks," said Larry, still trying not to run away in terror. "European style. Okay...we have to get going...thanks."

They moved deeper into the exhibit and came across an entire ancient tomb rebuilt inside the gallery. Three thick, stone walls were adorned in hieroglyphics and two ornate sarcophagi lay side by side in the middle of the reconstructed room.

Ahkmenrah spread his arms wide and sighed. "I haven't seen these walls in many a moon."

"Ahkmen!" said a woman's voice.

The group turned to see an ornately dressed Egyptian couple emerge from the shadows. The woman had dark hair, dark eyes, and wore a long thin gown with golden stitching. The shorter man wore a golden tunic and headpiece similar to that of Ahkmenrah. He held a tall, golden staff.

"Mother!" said Ahkmenrah. The woman ran over and hugged her son. Tears streamed down her cheeks.

Ahkmenrah released his mother and turned toward the man. "Father."

The man paused a bit awkwardly for a moment, then strode over to the young pharaoh. The older man wrapped his arms around his son and embraced him deeply. "Welcome home, my son."

Larry smiled as he watched the reunion. He glanced over at Nick and saw that his son was smiling, too. Nick's eyes caught Larry's and the boy's smile disappeared.

"I want you to meet my friends," said Ahkmenrah. He led the couple over to the group.

"I am Merenkahre, Pharaoh of the Nile and Father of the Son of the Sun," said Ahkmenrah's father.

"And I am Shepseheret, the Glittering Jewel of the Nine Kingdoms," said Ahkmenrah's mother.

Larry gave a small wave. "Hi. I'm Larry."

"Guardian of Brooklyn," finished Ahkmenrah.

Larry leaned toward the young pharaoh. "I actually live in Manhattan now," he whispered.

Ahkmenrah winced. "I know. But it doesn't sound as cool."

Larry stepped closer to Merenkahre. "Listen, I need to talk to you about the tablet."

The man stiffened. "You are speaking to a Pharaoh. Kiss my staff." He leaned the head of the staff toward Larry's face.

Larry politely moved it out of the way. "I'll pass."

Merenkahre glowered. "You will show respect. I am the descendant of Ra, the Sun God."

"Okay, I don't worship Ra, actually, so..." Larry began.

"The Egyptian Gods are the only true Gods," interrupted Ahkmenrah's father.

"Yeah, we try to stay open-minded," replied Larry. He jutted a thumb over his shoulder "Attila worships a sort of goat-god thing, so...we don't judge. I'm part Irish-Catholic, part Jewish..."

Merenkahre grinned. "You are? I love Jews!"

Ahkmenrah rubbed his temples. "Here we go."

"We owned forty thousand of them!" said his father.

Shepseheret beamed. "Such nice people."

"Father, that's not okay anymore," said Ahkmrenrah. "Owning people."

"What?" asked his father. "They were very happy. Always singing, with the candles."

"They weren't happy," Larry corrected. "They left. They actually walked through the Red Sea just to get out of there. We have dinner once a year and talk about it." He shook his head. "Listen, the tablet ...there's something wrong with it." Larry handed the tablet to Merenkahre.

The older pharaoh ran a hand over the green stain. He flipped some of the tiles, examining them closely. "It's losing its power." He shook his head. "I warned them not to move it. I specifically said, *The End Will Come!* How hard is that?"

"You have to help me fix it," said Larry.

Merenkahre raised an eyebrow. "To do that, I would have to divulge the secret of the tablet."

Larry nodded. "I promise I won't tell anyone."

The older pharaoh stared at the tablet in his hands. His brow furrowed.

"Father! Why do you insist on keeping this to yourself?" asked Ahkmenrah.

"The secret was to be passed down to you at the right time," Merenkahre explained.

"Well, now seems like a good time," said Ahkmenrah. "Father, please. I will always be your son, but I am also Pharaoh. I need to know. And I need to know now."

Merenkahre sighed. He held the tablet and leaned back on one of the sarcophagi. "You were born at midnight," he explained. "I was Pharaoh, and I had seen wonders most men only dream of. But when I first gazed upon you...I knew I could never bear to say goodbye." He exchanged a smile with his wife. "I commanded the high priest to prepare a gift for you ...using all we had learned from the mysteries of the Afterlife."

Merenkahre held up the tablet with both hands. "It was forged in the temple of Khonsu, God of the Moon and watcher over nighttime travelers...the Tablet of Ahkmenrah. The moon god bestowed his power upon the tablet. As long as it bathed in his light, our family could be together forever. Not even Death could part us." He ran his fingers over the green stain once more. "It has been away from Khonsu's light for far too long."

Just then, the tablet glowed green. Larry's friends staggered. Even the older Egyptians held their sides in pain.

Shepseheret's eyes widened. "My son!"

Ahkmenrah's face began to whither and crack. He was returning to his mummified form.

Merenkahre held out the tablet to Larry. "It needs moonlight. Let it be replenished with the power of Khonsu." He looked at his wife and son. "Otherwise we will all be dead by sunrise, never to breathe life again."

Larry took the tablet and ran toward the exit. "Nick, let's go." The boy followed and they sprinted through the Egyptian wing.

As they ran, something caught Larry's eye. He halted and turned back to the entrance of a large chamber. Several sarcophagi were on display, but they weren't what Larry had noticed. In the center of the round chamber, a single shaft of moonlight pierced the darkness. Larry and Nick entered and came to a stop in the center of the bright shaft.

Larry held up the tablet. Nothing happened. The moonlight washed over the golden artifact but the green stain remained. Then Larry noticed that several of the spinning tiles were askew. He quickly turned them back into place. He was about to spin the last one when something very cold and sharp touched his throat. Larry froze.

"I told you our paths would cross again," said a familiar voice. Larry cut his eyes to see Lancelot in the shadows. His long sword, however, pierced the moonlight and its tip rested on Larry's neck. "The tablet, please," said the knight.

Larry held his breath. "I don't think so."

"Oh, really?" asked the knight. The sword gleamed in the moonlight as it moved from Larry's throat to Nick's. "How about now?"

CHAPTER 8

Larry's job as a night guard was to protect the museum exhibits. To protect his friends. Restoring the tablet would restore his friends. His job would be complete. His mission would be a success. Larry's job as a father was to protect his son. He cringed at the sight of the sharp blade so close to Nick's throat. He knew that he had no choice. He handed the tablet to Lancelot.

The knight took the tablet with one hand but kept his sword trained on Nick. "King Arthur wasted years searching for the Holy Grail," Lancelot explained. "He was looking for a cup! And to think, it was a tablet all along. My quest is complete. I ride for Camelot tonight!"

"You have no idea what you're doing," Larry explained. "The tablet is dying," Larry pointed to the crooked tile. "You have to turn that middle piece right there."

Lancelot gave him a suspicious look. "You'd like that, wouldn't you?"

"Yeah." Larry nodded. "That's why I said it."

Lancelot rolled his eyes. "Sorry. It's not my first quest."

The knight shoved Nick aside and slammed the butt of his sword into Larry's gut. Larry doubled over in pain as the knight sheathed his sword and disappeared down the dark corridor.

"Dad!" yelled Nick.

Larry held his stomach, trying to catch his breath. "Get the others! We can't let him leave the museum!"

Nick ran back the way they had come, going after their friends. Trying to ignore the pain in his stomach, Larry lurched forward giving chase to the knight. Larry slowly built up speed as he followed the armored man's heavy footfalls. He chased Lancelot out of the Egyptian wing and down a main hallway. Living exhibits of all kinds scrambled out of the way as the foot chase wound through the museum halls.

Lancelot led Larry through gallery after gallery, trying to lose the night guard. Luckily, Larry had plenty of experience chasing living exhibits through museums. And honestly, keeping up with an armored knight was easier than keeping up with a monkey with a stolen key ring.

Larry pursued Lancelot into a gallery that was devoid of living exhibits. A quick glance told Larry that they were in an area dedicated to M.C. Escher. The artist was famous for his work depicting environments that defied the laws of gravity and physics. Around him the framed prints were alive with fish turning into ducks, men climbing never-ending stairs, and a sketch of a hand sketching a hand that was sketching the same hand.

Lancelot was almost on the other side of the gallery when the exit door flew open. Teddy stepped through, holding the largest rifle Larry had ever seen.

"Speak softly and carry a big stick," announced Teddy. He smiled down at his rifle. "1895 .375 H&H Magnum Elephant Gun. Turns out they have a rather nice collection here."

Lancelot slid to a stop as Teddy aimed the rifle at the man's armored chest. Larry slowed his run, trying to catch his breath before getting closer to the rogue knight. The mad chase was finally over. Teddy had Lancelot covered.

"Lawrence, we may have a problem," Teddy said nervously. He glanced at his gloved hands holding the rifle. Both of Teddy's hands had gone stiff. They had turned back to wax. The elephant gun fell out of his grasp and clattered to the floor.

Lancelot slowly unsheathed his sword, "I have a saying, too. Speak loudly and carry a *bigger* stick." He stepped toward Teddy, raising his blade, ready to strike.

Larry ran forward and sprung at the knight. He tackled Lancelot around the waist and hurled him away from Teddy. The two flew toward a large Escher print on the wall. Instead of slamming against the artwork, the two flew *into* it. Larry felt the same feeling he felt when he had entered a giant photograph at the Smithsonian. However, this time, as they crossed the threshold, his stomach lurched as he felt gravity pull at him from different directions.

At first, everything seemed normal. That is, normal for flying into a print brought to life by a magic tablet. Larry and Lancelot tumbled onto a stairway landing. Then the knight raised a boot and kicked Larry over the side. Instead of falling down, over the railing, he flew off to the side and stuck to a nearby wall. Larry stood on the wall and looked over to see Lancelot crouched on the landing, which was now sideways to Larry.

The vast space was crisscrossed with staircases, archways, and catwalks. Some were right-side up, some upside down, and others stretched sideways. They all met each other in the impossible ways the artist was famous for creating. Faceless figures easily marched along the insane steps and catwalks. The figures didn't react to the new arrivals. They kept marching along as if in a trance.

While Lancelot slowly got to his feet, Larry looked around for a way to cross over to the knight. Luckily, Larry didn't have to hurry. Lancelot was no sooner on his feet when Teddy flew into the environment. The stiff-armed president crashed into the knight, sending him tumbling back to the ground. As the knight pushed Teddy off him, the tablet slipped from his grasp. It went over the landing and tumbled down, out of sight.

Larry peered into the darkness, trying to see where the tablet went. Hearing a clank, Larry looked up to see the tablet enter from the opposite direction. It bounced down a staircase high above them. It came to rest on the lip of a step.

Lancelot raced up a set of stairs while Larry and Teddy looked for a way to cut him off.

Larry pointed to another set of stairs near Teddy. "You go that way, I'll go this way." Larry gestured at a thin catwalk. "I guess."

"This whole place is cattywampus!" said Teddy.

Lancelot was almost at the tablet when one of the faceless figures marched down and kicked it aside. The tablet flew off the side of the stairs, made a sharp right turn, and then clanked down the steps leading down a nearby wall. The knight roared with frustration and shoved the figure away from him.

Teddy ran up the sideways stairs, two steps from the tablet. "Got it!" shouted Teddy.

"Not quite," said Lancelot. The knight plunged feet-first off the landing. He took the same hard right turn as the tablet. His boots rammed into Teddy's chest, knocking the former president off the steps. Teddy hooked his stiff arms on the lip of the stairs and dangled as the knight flew out of sight.

To Larry, all of this looked as if it happened above him. The steps were directly overhead as he ran up matching stairs below. Instead of falling down, Teddy dangled straight up.

Larry took a deep breath and jumped up. He felt the gravity of the steps above him and he rolled in midair. Larry came crashing down on the steps where Teddy was hanging. Larry grabbed the tablet with one hand and Teddy's arm with the other. He strained to pull his friend to safety.

The blade of a dagger entered Larry's field of vision. "The tablet. Now," ordered Lancelot. The knight stood on the wall next to him. His dagger pointed at Larry's neck.

"Let me go, Lawrence," Teddy said calmly.

"I'm not going to let you go!" said Larry.

"I shan't ask you a third time, Fool," said the knight. He inched the tip of the blade closer to Larry's throat. "Give me the tablet."

Larry snarled. He was getting tired of blades being pointed at his neck.

Teddy smiled. "It's all right, Lawrence. Let go."

Larry gripped Teddy's wrist tighter. He could feel the stiff gloved hand sliding under his fingers. "No!"

Just before Teddy slipped free, the former president gave Larry a wink. "See you on the other side." Teddy fell from his grasp and plummeted into the darkness below.

"Teddy!" Larry shouted after him. He couldn't believe it. He had lost his friend.

Larry stood and faced his perpendicular foe. Reluctantly, he handed Lancelot the tablet. The knight grinned triumphantly.

Suddenly, Teddy Roosevelt, former Rough Rider and twenty-sixth president of the United States, flew in sideways. He slammed into Lancelot, sending the knight and the tablet flying. Larry caught Teddy's arm as he tumbled to a stop.

"Thought I lost you there, TR," said Larry.

Teddy smiled. "Me, too. I had no idea that would work."

As Larry helped Teddy to his feet, he glanced over the edge of the stairs. His heart sank as he saw Lancelot scoop up the tablet and head toward the front of the print—the portal back to the museum.

The knight dove through the opening and into the Escher gallery. He was full-sized once again and running away.

Octavius was truly amazed at the size of this museum. He, Jedediah, and Dexter had traveled its many corridors and still hadn't seen any sign of their friends. As expected, they had seen many wondrous creatures during their travels. Even now, they spotted a knight in gleaming armor running toward them with the golden Tablet of Ahkmenrah tucked under one arm. Octavius stopped in his tracks and drew his sword. What was that knight doing with *their* tablet?

Jedediah must have seen it, too. He halted and drew his six shooters. Dexter chirped angrily.

"Hold it right there, pardner!" Jedediah ordered.

The knight came to a stop in front of them. He glanced around, looking for the source of their voices. Finally, his eyes fell on the trio below. His brow furrowed as he gazed down at them.

"I don't know who you are," Jed continued. He waved one of his guns at the tablet. "But I'm pretty sure that there magic tablet don't belong to you."

Octavius aimed his sword at the knight. "You think you can come in here with your spectacularly good looks…" He gestured to the man's sword. "And your absolutely enormous sword, and just start stealing things?"

Dexter crossed his arms and snarled up at the man.

The knight didn't reply. Instead, he simply gave them a smile and casually stepped over them. The three turned and watched him continue running down the hall.

Octavius shrugged. "Apparently he was correct in that assumption."

Jedediah holstered his pistols and threw his hat on the ground. "Now that ain't right! You gotta at least engage in some way!" He turned to Octavius. "And he didn't even pretend to jump."

Octavius sheathed his sword and waved a fist at the retreating knight. "You'll rue the night you disrespected us, you beautiful man!"

More footsteps thundered behind them. Octavius turned to see Larry Daley and President Roosevelt running down the corridor. They stopped when they spotted the three on the floor.

"Good to see you guys," said Larry. "Oct, I think this belongs to you." He reached into his jacket pocket and pulled out a tiny piece of cloth. He bent down and offered it to Octavius. It was his scarlet cape. The roman commander affixed it to his armor.

"We tried, Gigantor," said Jed. "He ain't seen the last of us, that flaxen-maned scoundrel!"

More footsteps. The rest of their group ran up from an adjoining gallery. An older Egyptian couple was with them. Octavius guessed that they were Ahkmenrah's parents.

"I don't understand," said Teddy as he caught his breath. "Why is Lancelot staying strong while we get weaker?"

"Tonight's his first night," explained Ahkmenrah's father. "Newborns are stronger. But it matters not. Unless we succeed, he too will be dead come the dawn."

"All right, we don't have much time," said Larry. "We have to cover the exits." He pointed to the Egyptian couple. "You take Egypt, in case he comes back through there. Nicky, Atilla, Dex...cover India. Teddy, you and the others scout Mesopotamia." Larry jutted a thumb at himself. "I've got the main entrance."

Nick reached down and gently picked up Jed and Octavius. He placed them into his vest pocket and they were soon racing down the corridors, after the scoundrel.

Larry weaved past living exhibits as he made his way to the museum's main entrance. When he got there, he felt like he had been punched in the stomach…again. The main doors were wide open and Lancelot was already outside. The knight sat atop a large armored horse. The mighty steed whinnied as it reared its front hooves into the air. Larry could spot the tablet poking out of a pouch on the saddle. The knight locked eyes with Larry and smiled. The horse returned to the ground and Lancelot kicked at its sides with both heels. The stallion galloped across the courtyard and into the night.

Larry took off after him. He was no more than ten feet into the courtyard when someone blocked his path. It was Tilly, the British Museum's night guard. She had Laaa by one arm. The Neanderthal's hairy wrists were bound in front of him. They were tied together with a thick plastic tie. The caveman wore a sad expression of defeat.

"I knew you smelled a bit off," said Tilly.

Larry pointed over his shoulder. "You didn't just see a knight in shining armor go riding through here a second ago?"

"Don't try to distract me with your magical fantasy." Tilly nudged Laaa. "I found your filthy twin in the freight room."

"He's not my twin," said Larry. "I don't look anything like him."

"What are you talking about?" She looked from Larry to Laaa and then back to Larry. "You look exactly the same. That's how you fooled me. Doubles."

Larry didn't have time to argue. Lancelot was getting away, going who knows where. "I have to go."

Larry tried to edge around her but she brought up her hammer in a flash. "Whoops! You didn't see that coming, did you?" She wiggled the hammer. "Set up ... pay off, mate! So what's it gonna be? Heads?" She twisted the hammer around. "Or claws?"

Larry looked at the hammer, then back at Tilly. Maybe he could make a break for it.

"Weighing your odds?" asked Tilly. "Yeah ... brave gambit, but take care. Maybe I'm quicker than my frame suggests. Maybe inside this figure lives a jackrabbit." She waved the hammer. "You might get away. But if you do ..." She moved the hammer toward Laaa. "Your hideous doppelganger will pay the price."

Laaa looked up at Larry, his eyes full of remorse and fear. Larry shook his head and sighed.

CHAPTER 9

*B*AM!
Larry threw himself at the locked break-room door. It didn't even budge and all he had to show for it was a sore shoulder. Tilly had locked them inside. Laaa had chewed through his wrist restraints and was passing the time, sitting in a chair and beating his head against the table. All the while, the caveman moaned in shame.

"Don't beat yourself up, Laaa," consoled Larry. "It's not your fault."

Larry moved to the sink and picked up an old dishtowel. He wrapped it around his right fist and headed back to the door. They had to break out of there somehow. Larry reared back and punched the door's reinforced window. Nothing. Not even a crack.

"Argh!" Larry yelled in both frustration and pain.

This broke Laaa out of his head-banging trance. He moved to the door and punched it just as Larry did. "Aaaa!" Laaa yelled. He looked to Larry for approval.

"Laaa, if you see me do something dumb, don't imitate me, okay?" asked Larry.

The Neanderthal nodded.

Larry rubbed his aching hand. "That's basically what I keep telling Nick."

Laaa nodded again.

"It's a lot simpler for you, Laaa," said Larry. He moved throughout the room, searching through drawers and cabinets. Laaa followed him, listening intently. "All you have to do is worry about fire...no fire." Larry continued. "Shelter...no shelter." Larry found an old butter knife and marched back to the door. "The whole evolution thing? It just makes things more complicated."

Laaa followed Larry to the door, still listening and nodding.

"Look, I get it," said Larry. He pried at the lock with the tip of the butter knife. "I know where Nick is coming from. I'm just trying to help the kid skip twenty years of my mistakes."

Laaa pointed to the door and then to his head.

Larry frowned, trying to understand. "Door... head. Okay..."

Laaa reached out and opened an imaginary door. Then he pointed to his head again.

"Open your head?" asked Larry. Then his eyes widened. "Open your mind! Yeah, well, that's

130

parenting right there, Laaa." Larry nodded. "That's the challenge."

Laaa shook his head and gently moved Larry aside. He took a step back, lowered his head, and charged the door. His head rammed through the reinforced window, shattering the glass. Laaa pulled his head out and then reached through the break in the window. He unlatched the door from the other side and swung the door open.

"Oh! Open the door with your head," said Larry. He patted the caveman on the back. "Good job."

Larry and Laaa ran out of the break room and into the freight room. He had to stop Tilly from calling the police. Lucky for him, it looked as if someone beat him to it. He found the rest of his group waiting for him outside. The guard shack door was closed with a stool jammed underneath the handle. Larry could hear Tilly pounding on the door.

"You won't get away with this," said her muffled voice. "I'm doing sketches of you in my mind!"

Larry ran up to his friends. "Everybody okay?"

"Yes, Lawrence," replied Teddy. "We've secured the lady guard in her booth. But I don't know how long that'll hold her."

"All right." Larry clasped his hands together. "We need to find Lancelot, but somebody has to keep that guard locked up."

Laaa stepped solemnly forward.

Larry nodded. "Laaa. You know what to do."

The caveman held up both hands, palms out, as if he were holding up an invisible door.

Larry smiled. "Make sure she stays in there."

Laaa nodded vigorously. "STAAAY!"

Larry pat him on the back. "Good." Laaa ran toward the guardhouse.

"Lawrence, I can't move my arms," said Teddy. Both of his arms were now frozen stiff. His hands jutted out from the elbows as if he were trying to shake two hands at once. "I fear we are becoming less useful by the minute."

Larry looked at the others. Sacajawea was almost expressionless. She was reverting back to her original plastic form. Ahkmenrah's face was even more aged and cracked. As Larry looked at Attila, the Hun warrior swayed and then dropped to his knees.

Larry rushed to help him to his feet. "Come on, big guy." Once the Hun was upright, Larry noticed that one of Attila's eyes had turned back to glass. It stared up and to the left. "Wow, you're looking all crazy-eyed there, man," said Larry. "Like, way more than normal."

Attila's lower lip jutted out. He seemed about to cry.

Larry grabbed his arm. "Just hang tough," Larry told him. "Listen to me. When does a Hun give up?"

Attila took a breath and summoned a brave smile. "Nagor."

"That's right. Nagor," said Larry. "He just keeps...pillaging and looting until the very last village is burned."

Larry turned to gaze at the London skyline. "Lancelot's out there somewhere."

"Dad, there's like eight million people in this city," said Nick. "The guy could be anywhere."

"We'll find him," said Larry. "We have to."

"Always the optimist, Leonard," said Teddy.

"Larry," corrected Larry.

Teddy nodded. "Right."

Larry led the way as they trekked into the heart of the city. As the strange group moved down the busy sidewalks, Larry tried to ignore the curious looks they received from passersby. He had to stay focused on tracking down the rogue knight. Surprisingly, they didn't get as many stares as he had expected. Then again, London was a big city. And if it were anything like living in New York, then the people were used to seeing all kinds of strange things every day.

When they came to a small park, Sacajawea knelt and examined the ground. "He came this way," she said through her tightening lips. "Traveling half an acre per hour. The horse...its left flank is weak."

They followed the trail for two blocks until it went cold. Then someone screamed from around a corner. That scream told Larry that they were still on the right trail.

"Come on," Larry said as they dashed down the sidewalk.

They turned the corner and saw Trafalgar Square spread out before them. The huge open space was surrounded by ornate granite buildings and had a large fountain near the center. Larry recognized the London landmark at once. It was named after a British naval victory during the Napoleonic Wars. It featured a two-hundred-foot column displaying a statue of the hero of that battle, Admiral Nelson. Surrounding the column were four bronze lion statues, each one the size of an SUV. *Normally*, the lions surrounded the column. Since Lancelot had come through with the magic tablet, awakening the statues, the lions now terrorized the square's many tourists.

As soon as Larry and the others entered the square, one of the lions turned its attention to them. It bared a mouthful of sharp bronze teeth.

ROOOOAR!

The other three lions noticed the first one's cry. They ceased their prowling and bounded over to join the first. Now all four lions snarled as they stalked the small group from New York. Ears back and teeth bared, they crept closer, ready to pounce.

"Lawrence? Ideas?" asked Teddy.

Jed and Octavius peeked out from a pocket in Nick's vest. "Use your flashlight, Gigantor," yelled Jed. "These cats want to play!"

Larry whipped out his flashlight and switched it on. He aimed the beam at the ground in front of the first lion. Its ears shot forward and its head darted down as it began tracking the lit circle. Larry wiggled the flashlight a bit, making the circle dance about. The lion reached out a paw, trying to catch the circle of light. When it couldn't stop the light from moving, it grabbed at it with both paws. Soon, the other lions joined the first. They all chased the light beam like kittens chasing the red dot of a laser pointer—just like one of Jed and Octavius' favorite Internet videos.

"Gigantor, get your phone out!" said Jed. "We gotta video this!"

"We don't have time for that," said Larry.

"By the barnacled brow of Neptune," said Octavius, shaking his head. "We'd have millions of hits."

Larry switched off the flashlight and slid it back onto his belt. He smiled at the romping lions. "This *would* be huge."

The lions continued to play like giant kittens. They pounced on each other and wrestled around the square. The tourists who hadn't run for their lives were busy taking pictures of the frisky felines.

They had solved that problem, but they were still no closer to catching Lancelot. Larry scanned the large square and saw no sign of the knight on horseback.

Teddy glanced around. "Where the devil did he go?"

Larry's eyes landed on a bus shelter. A large advertisement had been installed on one side. Larry smiled. He read the colorful poster and knew *exactly* where Lancelot was going.

CHAPTER 10

The bus pulled to a stop in front of the Palladium Theatre. Larry and the others filed off the vehicle amid the stares and occasional picture snaps of the other bus patrons. He had to admit that they must have been a strange sight. After all, how often did one see a Native American woman, Hun warlord, former U.S. president, Egyptian pharaoh, two living miniature figurines, and a monkey riding public transportation? And it wasn't even Halloween.

As the bus pulled away, Larry stared up at the grand theater. Ironically, its tall marble columns and wide steps looked quite similar to the Museum of Natural History back in New York. Larry felt a pang of homesickness.

Three things let them know that they had come to the right place. The first thing was a colorful banner that hung over the entrance. It announced the production currently going on inside. It was

Camelot, the musical. The popular play featured all the mythical characters from ancient lore. King Arthur, Queen Guinevere, and Sir Lancelot himself. The second thing was the armored horse milling about in front of the theater. That was a clue. But the thing that really let Larry know that they were in the right place was on the theater steps themselves. The steps were covered with a steady stream of panicked audience members. They screamed and shouted as they exited the theater.

Larry sighed. "I think we found him."

Like fish swimming upstream, Larry and his friends wove their way through the departing crowd. They made their way into the lobby and up the ramp to the theater itself. When they entered, Larry was taken aback by the huge space. Two rows of balconies encircled the seating on the main floor. Enormous velvet curtains decorated the theater and framed the large stage ahead.

Larry and his friends pushed through the crowded aisle toward the main stage. As he moved past the frightened people, he could just make out three figures on the stage. They stood near a set piece depicting the front of a regal castle. Torches affixed to the castle wall flickered light over the scene. The woman wore a flowing medieval gown while a man was dressed in a sparkling tunic and a golden crown.

They were obviously actors playing King Arthur and Queen Guinevere. The third figure wasn't acting at all. Larry recognized the armored figure of Lancelot at once. Thanks to the acoustics of the theater, Larry could hear every word the knight said.

"I am Lancelot!" announced the knight. "I've fulfilled my quest, Arthur. I carry the treasure you sought but never could find." He pulled the tablet from a pouch and held it high. "The key to life everlasting!"

The actress moved closer to the man playing King Arthur. She pointed to her head, making small circles with her finger. "His cream's gone lumpy."

Lancelot pointed to the castle set. "And look what you've done! Camelot used to inspire the hearts of men." The knight slid the tablet back into his pouch and drew his sword. "You've turned it into a gaudy puppet show!" Lancelot hacked at a nearby bush. The flat wooden set piece was sliced in half.

Larry and the others pushed closer to the stage.

"Do you know how long I've dreamed of coming home?" asked Lancelot. "And for what? Some tawdry deception?"

In one blow, he cut down a two dimensional tree. He slammed the butt of his sword into the trunk, hurling it into the audience. The few theatergoers who were left in their seats scattered as the set piece flew their way. They fled up the aisle, slowing Larry and the others' progress further.

"You don't deserve your crown, Arthur," said Lancelot. He aimed his sword at the actor. "And you don't deserve your queen!"

"I'm not a queen," said the woman playing Guinevere.

"That's right," agreed the man playing Arthur. "She's an actor. So am I." He held out his hands to the set around them. "This is all just pretend, mate."

"It's not real," added the woman.

"Lancelot!" shouted Larry. He and the others ran up to the edge of the stage. "Leave them out of this. It's not their fight."

The actor playing Arthur jutted a thumb toward the knight. "You know this guy?"

Larry sighed and nodded. "Yeah."

Lancelot looked from Larry and his friends to the actors and the set of Camelot. His face fell and he turned and ran. The knight snatched a torch from the fake castle wall and disappeared backstage.

Larry led the way as he and his friends ran up the stairs and atop the stage. They ran past the two actors and into the wings. Once backstage, Larry found a spiral staircase. He heard footsteps above.

Larry and the others climbed the stairs until they reached a landing and a door leading to the roof. Larry opened the door and dashed outside. He spotted Lancelot standing near the edge of the roof, his back to them. It had begun to snow and large flakes drifted down over the knight.

"Hey, give me the tablet!" ordered Larry.

The knight spun and brandished the torch. "Back off!"

Larry held up his hands in defense but he stepped closer. "It's over."

"Back!" ordered the knight. He stepped forward, jabbing the torch at Larry.

Larry's eyes widened. "Whoa!" The torch had melted the knight's nose. Its tip dangled from the knight's face like a floppy little elephant's trunk. "What's up with your nose?" asked Larry.

"What? What's wrong with my nose?" Lancelot dropped the torch into an empty flower pot and his hands shot to his face. His fingers felt the drooping piece of wax. "Is it bad?"

"Yeah...no...it's all right," Larry replied. "I mean...it's not great."

Lancelot drew his sword. Larry braced himself, but the knight merely stared at his reflection in the gleaming blade. "But...I'm Lancelot."

Larry stepped forward. "Look, there never was a Lancelot. It's just a legend. You're a museum exhibit.

The tablet brought you to life, too...just like all the others you saw tonight."

The knight looked up from the sword. "I don't understand."

"I'm sorry man. I know that's hard to hear. But right now, you really have to give me the tablet. Please."

"And what then?" asked the knight, his eyes full of sadness. "Back to the museum? To stand there as little children ogle...and point?"

"And learn," Teddy added. "And get inspired to do great things of their own." Teddy smiled. "There are less noble fates, my friend."

"Not for me." The knight shook his head. "If there is no Camelot...if there is no Guinevere...and no Lancelot. Then I'm nothing. Just a sad lump of wax." His eyes flashed as he glared at Larry. "And stop looking at my nose!"

Larry held up his hands. "I wasn't."

"You were! I saw you," said Lancelot. He leaned forward, making his nose flop even more. "You were like this...uhhh...staring."

Larry shrugged. "Well, what do you want me to do?" He pointed at the knight's face. "It's all..."

"Don't say it," barked Lancelot. "Don't mention it and don't look at it."

Larry looked up at the sky. "I'll try not to look at it." His eyes found their way back to Lancelot's nose.

"Look at some other part of me," ordered the knight. He held up his hands. "No one look at or mention my nose from this moment forward!"

Larry looked away. Nick, Teddy, and Sacajawea looked away. Attila's crazy eye was already looking away.

"Now," said Lancelot. His brow furrowed. "I forgot what we were talking about."

Attila grunted as he fell to his knees. Teddy went stiff and fell flat on his face. Sacajawea tried to say something, but her mouth was completely sealed. She put Dexter down and moved toward Teddy.

"Larry," said Ahkmenrah. The young pharoah's face cracked and began to crumble. "We've run out of time."

Larry spotted the miniatures in Nick's pocket. Jed and Octavius could hardly move.

"Lancelot. Come on, man." Larry stepped toward the confused knight. "Listen to me. The tablet needs moonlight now. Otherwise my friends will die. And so will you."

Lancelot closed his eyes. "A world without Camelot is not a world worth living in."

"Dad!" shouted Nick.

Larry spun around to see Dexter wheezing and grabbing at his little furry chest. The monkey took two steps forward and collapsed at Larry's feet.

"Dex!" shouted Larry. He knelt beside the capuchin. "Come on, buddy! It's gonna be okay!"

Dexter's eyes dulled and his wheezing slowed. Larry was desperate. He slapped the little monkey's face. "Slap me back!" He moved his cheek closer to the monkey. "It's me! Larry! Come on, slap me!"

Dexter raised a feeble, tiny monkey hand toward Larry's face but then froze.

Larry put two fingers on Dexter's chest and began giving chest compressions. "One, two, three, four, five!" He leaned over and gave the monkey mouth-to-mouth resuscitation. It wasn't working.

Larry pounded on Dexter's chest. "Come on, Dex! Don't you quit on me, monkey! Fight, monkey! Fight!"

Tears welled up in Larry's eyes. Dexter couldn't be gone. The little monkey couldn't be dead.

"Enough, Lawrence," said Teddy. Sacajawea had him rolled over onto his side.

Larry looked over at his stiffening friend. "I can save him!"

"There's nothing you can do," Teddy said with a weak smile. "He's gone."

CHAPTER 11

Larry sat on the roof, slowly stroking Dexter's fur. He lightly brushed a fresh snowflake from the monkey's still face. He couldn't believe the little troublemaker was gone. Larry had failed him. He had failed all his friends.

Larry gazed at his dying friends. Although Teddy's eyes were still trained on him, it was clear that the former president could no longer move. Sacajawea was nearly frozen as well, her skin glossy and artificial. Attila still slumped in a heap, while Ahkmenrah was thin, withered, and cracked. It looked as if a strong gust could blow his body to dust.

Larry caught Nick's pleading eyes. Tears streamed down the boy's cheeks as he glanced down at his pocket. Octavius stiffly held his sword high, reverting back to his lead form. Jedediah was not far behind.

"It's been a heck of a ride, Gigantor." Jed struggled to get the words out.

Larry stood and turned to Lancelot. To Larry's surprise, the knight had tears in his eyes, too. He pointed down at Dexter. "You truly cared for that chimpanzee, didn't you?"

Larry's lip trembled. "He's a capuchin. He was my friend."

Lancelot smiled. "I understand now. The monkey *was* the quest." He pulled the tablet from his pouch. "A more noble quest than mine. It was never about the tablet. It was about them." He handed it to Larry. "Forgive me. It is I who have been the fool."

"Thank you," said Larry.

He turned the tablet over in his hands. The once golden Tablet of Ahkmenrah was now dull, green, and corroded. His fingers ran over the askew tile. The corrosion made it difficult to turn at first. But with a little effort, Larry clicked it back into place. He examined it in the moonlight. Nothing happened. It was too late. The tablet was powerless.

Tears filled Larry's eyes, blurring his vision. As he wiped them away, he noticed that the tablet didn't seem as dull anymore. In fact, the green stain began fading away. Larry shut his eyes as the tablet flashed a brilliant golden light.

Attila gasped as he sat upright. Teddy jolted up and began moving again. Sacajawea took in a deep breath, finally able to open her mouth. The cracks in Ahkmenrah's face faded and a wide smile stretched across his face. Larry and Nick laughed as both Jedediah and Octavius took in deep breaths.

There was a loud screech at Larry's feet. He looked down just in time to see Dexter leaping up at him. Larry caught the grinning monkey in his arms.

"Welcome back, Dex!" said Larry.

Everyone was back. Nick, Attilla, and Ahkmenrah were laughing. Teddy and Sacajawea hugged, and Jedediah and Octavius were jumping for joy in Nick's pocket. Dexter leaped out of Larry's arms to join the others.

Larry smiled and his eyes filled with tears once more. But this time, they were tears of joy. He had done it. He had saved them all. He ran over to hug his friends. To hug his son.

When Larry finally let go, he turned back to see Lancelot standing by the edge of the roof. His back was to them as he gazed out at the city. As Larry approached him, he saw the knight pull the silk scarf from his gauntlet. He ran a finger over the embroidered image of Camelot.

"It was just so beautiful in my head," said the knight. "I wanted it to last forever."

"I get it, man," said Larry. "Believe me." Larry turned back to gaze at his friends. At his son.

Lancelot closed his eyes and held the scarf to his face once more. He inhaled deeply. With a light smile, he raised the silken cloth high into the air. He released the scarf and it fluttered away in a swirl of snowflakes. It floated up into the moonlit sky until it disappeared into darkness.

After a moment of contemplation, the knight held up his sword to check himself in its reflecting surface. He used his other hand to mush his melted nose back into shape. When he was finished, he sheathed his sword and turned to face Larry and the others. He stood tall, his nose perfect once more.

"How do I look?" asked the knight.

Larry smiled. "You look like Lancelot."

When Larry and the others returned to the museum, they headed straight for the Egyptian wing. Upon entering the familiar tomb, Ahkmenrah's mother and father rushed over to embrace their son.

After their joyous reunion, Merenkahre strode over to Larry and put a hand on his shoulder. "Thank you for bringing my son home safely," said the older pharaoh. "You can't possibly know the worry that was in my heart."

Larry looked over at Nick and smiled. "I think I have a vague idea."

Merenkahre followed Larry's gaze. "It's a strange thing to see your boy become a man."

Larry sighed. "Yeah. One minute they're riding a dinosaur in Central Park, the next minute they're DJ-ing in Ibiza."

Ahkmenrah's father nodded with a blank stare, clearly not understanding what Larry had just said. Then a wide grin spread across Merenkahre's face. "You have served my family well. We will build a great tomb and bury you with many riches." His eyes widened. "I will personally see to it that your organs are removed and placed in separate jewel-encrusted jars."

Larry cringed. "Thank you?"

Merenkahre patted Larry on the shoulder and rejoined his family.

"Lawrence, if we might have a word," said Teddy. The group moved in close. Teddy glanced at the others. "We have been talking and..."

"And Ahkmenrah's place is here with his family," Octavius finished. He and Jed stood on the floor next to the others. "The young pharaoh must remain here."

Larry nodded. It made perfect sense. After all, Ahkmenrah's parents had not seen their son for thousands of years. Who was he to break up such a happy reunion? His mind began to race with different ways that he and Dr. McPhee could make that happen.

Teddy gave a sympathetic smile. "The tablet should stay here as well, lad."

Larry's eyes widened. He didn't see that one coming. "But…" he began.

"The tablet belongs to them," Sacajawea interrupted.

"This is where it belongs, Gigantor," agreed Jed. "Where it has always belonged."

Larry looked at Ahkmenrah and his family. They truly seemed happy. The young pharaoh caught his eye and strode over to join Larry and the others.

Larry turned back to the group. "Then…you guys are going to have to stay here, too," he said. "That's the only way."

Ahkmenrah nodded. "You would be most welcome."

"You're very kind," said Sacajweah. "But we belong in New York."

Attila nodded in agreement. .

Larry couldn't believe his ears. "But…you won't be…alive anymore."

"We never expected to be alive once," Teddy explained. He smiled at Sacajawea. "I've had sixty good years, Lawrence."

150

"Yeah, Gigantor," agreed Jed. "We're museum exhibits. Kids come to look at us, maybe learn a little somethin'— that's as alive as I need to be."

"But I'm supposed to take care of you guys," said Larry.

Teddy put a hand on Larry's shoulder. "And you have." He nodded. "It's okay, Lawrence. We're ready."

Larry gave a weak smile. "I'm not."

"Let us go." Teddy nodded. "It's time."

Larry's gaze moved over their faces. He couldn't believe this was the end. He caught Nick's eye and then realized that everything he loved most in life was right there in that room. He didn't know how he could let them go—all of them. However, deep down in his heart, he realized what his friends had already come to know. He knew it was the right thing to do. Finally, Larry nodded in agreement.

"Well, that settles it," said Teddy. He reached out and shook Ahkmenrah's hand. "King, it has been an honor and a pleasure."

"The pleasure has been mine, Mr. President," said the young pharaoh. He turned to Larry. "Thank you for everything, Larry, Guardian of Brooklyn."

Larry smiled. "You're right. It has a good ring to it."

Larry looked down at the tablet. He ran his fingers over the ancient symbols one last time. The tablet had not only brought his friends to life but it had changed Larry's life forever. It truly was magical. He handed it to Ahkmenrah.

"Goodbye, my friends," said Ahkmenrah.

"Dad, if we leave now, we can catch a flight," Nick suggested. "We could get home with everyone still alive before the sun comes up."

Larry put an arm around Nick's shoulder. "Good idea."

Larry led the way for the last time as they exited the Egyptian wing. Once outside, he spotted Lancelot waiting for them. The knight stood beside the now docile Triceratops skeleton. The fossilized creature wagged its tail as Lancelot scratched the side of its skull.

"Whoa," said Nick. "How did you do that?"

Lancelot smiled. "It's amazing what you can get done with some liver snaps and the business end of a broadsword."

"Someone once told me a true knight protects and cares for those in need," Larry said as he marched forward. "Can I count on you?"

Lancelot smiled and gave a small bow. "It shall be an honor."

They said their goodbyes to the knight and made their way back to the freight room. While Nick helped the others repack themselves into the large crate, Larry stepped outside to retrieve Laaa. Once outside, he saw that the guard shack door was wide open. The caveman was nowhere to be found.

"Unbelievable," Larry said as he broke into a run.

He reached the open door and looked inside. He couldn't believe what he saw. Tilly sat on a stool with Laaa sitting on the ground in front of her. The caveman had his back to her as he chowed down on packing peanuts. Tilly was talking a mile a minute as she braided the Neanderthal's shaggy hair.

"With Tarquin it's all a pose," she said. "He's a good guy, but he's so busy trying to be a *gangsta*. With the chains...and the grill...and the sidey-ways hat that makes him look like a small child. He never really listened." She stroked one of Laaa's matted locks. "Not like you. You really listen...with your heart."

Larry closed his gaping mouth and shook his head. "Uh, hi. Sorry to interrupt. Laaa, the guys are waiting for us."

Laaa rose to leave but Tilly took his hand. "Stay. We could make a life together. Away from judgment and labels. Please."

Laaa gave her a smile and gently caressed her cheek with the back of his hairy hand.

Tilly's eyes filled with tears. "I'll never forget you." She took his hand and gently kissed it. Laaa stepped out of the booth, letting his hand slowly slip from her grasp.

Larry had to close his gaping mouth again. He began to follow Laaa but then stopped. He turned back to the booth and peeked his head in. Tilly looked heartbroken.

"Hey, listen," said Larry. "I know that you hate your job...and tonight was kind of weird." Larry glanced around and leaned closer. "But tomorrow night..." He grinned. "Best job ever."

CHAPTER 12

Nick had been right. Because of the time difference, the New York group had flown back to the United States all through the night. By the time they had reached the museum, there was just under an hour left before sunrise. Everyone had made it back just fine—everyone except Ahkmenrah and the tablet.

While Larry's friends returned to their various displays, he went downstairs and cleaned out his locker. He stuffed all of his belongings into a duffle bag. Then, as he pulled out a pair of old sneakers, he spotted some tattered pages on the bottom of the locker. He pulled out the papers and smiled. It was his original instructions from when he first started. One of the previous night guards, Cecil, had given them to him when Larry first took the job. The pages had been taped and stapled back together from his first few misadventures in the museum. The writing was faded but he could still make out the first thing on the list. *Throw the bone*. Larry smiled and placed the pages back into the locker. He shut the door.

Larry swung by the Egyptian wing. He wanted to check it out one last time. No doubt it would be remodeled since the star attraction would no longer be there. As Larry entered the main gallery, he was surprised to see Dexter sitting on the railing. The little monkey stared up at the empty space where the golden Tablet of Ahkmenrah had been on display.

"It's weird not having it here," said Larry.

The monkey chirped in agreement. He looked up at Larry with sad eyes.

Larry checked his watch. "Well, almost dawn, buddy. You'd better get back over to Africa."

Dexter lowered his head. He began to climb down but Larry stopped him.

"Listen, when you almost...you know, up on that roof," said Larry. "I just want you to know it gave me a new perspective. I know we've always had our whole weird dynamic, but I just want to say...I appreciate you."

Dexter grinned up at Larry. Then the monkey reared back, ready to deliver a monster of a slap.

Larry leaned forward. "It's okay. One last slap."

Instead of striking, Dexter reached up and pulled Larry's head down. The mischievous capuchin, the troublemaker of the museum, the stealer of key rings …gave Larry a quick kiss on the lips. Dexter hopped down and scampered out of the gallery.

Larry frowned. "I just wish I'd taught you how to brush."

The next stop was the Hun exhibit. When Attila spotted Larry, he struggled to keep it together. The warrior's lip quivered and his eyes filled with tears.

Larry nodded. "It's okay, Attila. Let it out."

The Hun warlord blubbered as tears streaked his cheeks. He threw his arms around Larry and sobbed into the night guard's shoulder.

Larry patted him on the back. "I'm going to miss you, too, big fella." Attila cried louder and squeezed Larry tighter. "Okay…ow!" Larry grunted. "You're actually hurting me a little."

Attila reluctantly let go and took a step back. He looked Larry in the eye. "Larry Daley kaska," he said. Then he pointed to his heart. "Attila zoscar."

Larry still didn't speak Hun but he knew exactly what the warlord meant. "Attila kaska," Larry replied. He pointed to his own heart. "Larry Daley zoscar." He'd keep Attila in his heart, too.

At the Neanderthal exhibit, Larry found Laaa milling around in front of his frozen companions. Laaa's face lit when he saw Larry approach.

"Laaa...I feel like we've been through a lot, emotionally, in just one night." Larry tussled the caveman's shaggy hair. "It's...genuinely hard to know what to say."

Laaa rubbed his hands together nervously and looked down. He seemed to study the floor for a bit. Then he looked up and his primitive eyes met Larry's. "Dada?"

Larry rolled his eyes. "Sure," he said. "Dada. Sort of."

Laaa gave a wide grin showing off his stained, crooked teeth. Then his smile slowly morphed to a mournful expression. "Staaaaay?"

Larry sighed. "I can't, buddy."

Laaa gave an accepting nod. Then he reached into his loincloth and pulled out one final packing peanut. He offered it to Larry. The night guard reluctantly accepted the foam nugget. Laaa looked at him, expecting Larry to eat it.

Larry held it up. "I'm going to save this for later."

From the Neanderthal display, Larry swung by the diorama room. He found Jedediah and Octavius standing on the edge of their display case. All around them, various miniature historical scenes were frozen in place.

"I thank you, in advance, for deleting my photos off the front-desk computer," said Octavius. "I wouldn't want them to fall into enemy hands."

"I'll take care of it," said Larry. He shook his head. "I can't believe I'm never going to see you guys again."

"Nonsense." Octavius waved away the notion. "You know right where to find us."

"Each and every day, Gigantor," Jed added. "Except for Thanksgiving and Christmas. We'll be here."

"You know what I'm going to remember most about you two?" asked Larry.

"What's that?" asked Jedediah.

Larry grinned. "How big you guys are."

Both miniatures stood straighter and puffed out their chests.

"We *are* big." Octavius agreed. "Compared to a flea...or a bacterium."

The tiny cowboy took off his hat and slapped it against the Roman's armored chest. "He means we're big in spirit," said Jed.

"Yes, I understand that," agreed Octavius. "I'm just saying both are true."

Larry turned to leave.

"Hey, Gigantor," Jed called out. "Would you do one last thing for us?"

Larry turned back and leaned close. "Anything."

"Get us down from here," said Jed. "It's way too high for little guys like us."

Larry carefully placed each one of the figurines back into their displays. Once again, Octavius commanded a legion of frozen centurions. Jedediah was back atop his horse overseeing the construction of a railroad line. Larry gave them one last wave before exiting the diorama gallery.

When Larry entered the main hall, he spotted a tender moment between Teddy and Sacajawea. They held each other close, gazing into each other's eyes. Teddy leaned close and whispered something into her ear. Sacajawea smiled, then whispered something into Teddy's ear. Then they held each other close and kissed.

Larry glanced around, trying to give the couple their privacy. When he turned back, Sacajawea was walking away. She spotted Larry and gave him a grateful smile. She raised one hand in farewell and Larry returned the gesture.

Teddy strolled over to Larry, glancing back to watch Sacajawea leave. "Whoever would have thought?" asked Teddy. "I'm wax. She's polyurethane. But somehow it worked."

Larry stared at the former president. It was difficult to put his feelings into words. "So…this is it, huh?"

"I suppose so," replied Teddy. "It's time for your next adventure." The former president flashed his trademark wide grin. "And I know young Nick is going to do great things."

They turned and strolled over to Teddy's display. "Yeah, he's ready to take on the world. All by himself."

"Then you've done your job," said Teddy.

They stopped when they reached Teddy's frozen horse. "You know, Lawrence, some men are born great, others have greatness thrust upon them..."

Larry rolled his eyes. "I know, I know..." It was the same advice Teddy had given him during his first night at the museum.

Teddy held up a finger. "Let me finish." He took that finger and pointed at Larry's chest. "You, my friend, have proven yourself to be something even more rare than a great man. You're a *good* man, Lawrence. It's been an extraordinary journey and I shall never forget you."

They stared at each other for a moment before giving each other a farewell hug. Teddy patted Larry twice on the back and released him. The twenty-sixth president of the United States climbed onto his horse and drew his saber.

"I have no idea what I'm going do tomorrow," said Larry.

Teddy's eye's sparkled. "How exciting." He gave Larry a wink and then raised his sword high, getting into position.

The light from the rising sun filled the windows. The warm glow washed over Rexy, the front desk, and the entire main hall. Larry looked at Teddy and saw him as a wax mannequin, frozen in place. Larry's wild adventure in the museum was over.

"Bully!" shouted Teddy.

Larry started, jumping back.

Teddy roared with laughter. "I gotcha! Still works after all these years!"

Larry held his chest. His heart raced but he chuckled at the joke. "You got me...again." Then Larry's smile faded. "Hey Teddy?"

"Yes?" asked the former president.

"Thank you," said Larry.

Teddy smiled. "You're welcome." Then he cocked his head. "Smile, my boy." He turned to look out the main windows. "It's sunrise."

Larry followed his gaze and saw the first sun rays burst through the windows. It was beautiful. He turned back and saw that Teddy was frozen in place. Now, it was truly over.

Larry picked up his bag and headed for the main doors. He glanced back one last time before stepping outside. He inhaled the crisp winter air and it truly felt like a new day. Nick was sitting halfway down the main steps. Larry dropped his bag and sat beside him.

"You okay?" asked Nick.

"You know what?" asked Larry. "Yeah...I am."

Nick looked over his shoulder. "I'm going to miss this place."

"Yeah," Larry nodded. "Me, too."

They sat in silence watching traffic go by. Bundled up pedestrians filled the sidewalks and dog-walkers crisscrossed Central Park across the street.

"So," Larry said, breaking the silence. "Ibiza."

"Yeah, look, that whole DJ thing," Nick sighed. "I don't know if that's the thing for me. I just know it's the *next* thing." Nick shrugged. "I'm just ...figuring it out. You know?"

Larry nodded. "Sounds like a plan."

Nick laughed. "Heck of an adventure, Dad."

Larry nodded. "It was."

"I should get back to Mom's." Nick set off down the sidewalk. Larry stood and watched him go. He knew he couldn't watch out for him forever. Just like his friends at the museum, he'd have to let him go soon. Nick was no longer his little boy. He was well on his way to being a man. *A good man,* Larry thought.

"They grow up fast, don't they?" asked a voice behind him. Dr. McPhee stepped up beside him. They both watched Nick disappear into the crowd. "I'm childless, personally," McPhee continued. "Happily so."

Larry turned to see the disheveled museum director. He wore the same suit and topcoat he'd been wearing the last time they were together. McPhee's hair was a mess and there were stains on his coat and trousers.

McPhee noticed Larry's stare. "Well, I spent the night in the reservoir," McPhee explained.

Larry cocked his head. "Why?"

McPhee shrugged. "I didn't know what else to do. Been wandering the park all night."

Larry frowned. "That sounds...unwise."

"It was," agreed McPhee. He sighed. "Regrets ...I have a few." Then he clapped his hands together. "Your mission. Was it a success?"

"Yeah. It was," replied Larry.

McPhee waved a hand at the front of the museum. "So everything will go back to the way it was before?"

Larry shook his head. "Not the way it was. But that's okay. Ahkmenrah and the tablet are on permanent loan to the British Museum."

McPhee's jaw dropped. "You don't...remotely have the authority to do that."

Larry grinned. "Yeah, but you will. I'm going to tell Dr. Phelps that the whole planetarium disaster was my fault. I'll convince her to give you back your job."

"But then she'll just fire you," said Dr. McPhee. "What good would that do?"

"That's okay," replied Larry. "It's time to move on." Larry dug out his museum key ring and handed it over to Dr. McPhee. He pulled the flashlight from his belt and offered that up, too.

"I don't actually need a flashlight," said McPhee. "I'm not going to be a security guard. I have loads of lamps in my office. I'm over-lamped."

Larry waved the light. "It's symbolic."

McPhee nodded and accepted the flashlight. "Best left unsaid. Emotions. Feelings. Right then." He gave Larry a small smile and then climbed the steps, toward the museum.

Larry picked up his bag and headed down the sidewalk. It was a beginning of a new day and he really didn't know what he was going to do next. He smiled as he remembered what Teddy had told him. It *was* exciting.

Three years later, Dr. McPhee stood on the same steps where he last spoke with Larry Daley. The snow had long since melted away and Central Park was lush and green. The doctor had no idea what Larry was up to lately. Frankly, he didn't care. Larry did make good on his promise to take full responsibility for the planetarium fiasco. McPhee had been reinstated as museum director, and he had filed the necessary paperwork to have Ahkmenrah and his tablet transferred to the British Museum. He had even sweetened the deal by shipping over the pharaoh's sarcophagus and other artifacts from his tomb. The young pharaoh's new home was officially now in McPhee's mother country—England.

That was...until now.

Dr. McPhee gazed up at the banners adorning the front of the museum. A large image of the Tablet of Ahkmenrah adorned one banner while an image of the pharaoh's jeweled sarcophagus was on the other.

"For a limited time only," he read the banners. "King Ahkmenrah returns!"

Dr. McPhee climbed the steps to the museum. The artifacts were being installed that night and tomorrow was the opening day.

Okay, McPhee cared a *little* about Mr. Daley's current whereabouts. As a courtesy, he had tried contacting the former night guard, letting him know that the tablet and the pharaoh's mummified remains were visiting. After all, Mr. Daley had been going on about the tablet being magical and how it brought all the exhibits to life each night.

McPhee laughed at the thought. "The tablet glows," he said in his best Larry Daley impersonation.

The museum director walked briskly to the Egypt wing. He entered Ahkmenrah's display just as the workers were finishing installing the exhibit. One man wiped down the sarcophagus while another carefully removed the tablet from a wooden crate. He carefully flicked packing peanuts from the golden tiles.

Dr. McPhee glanced at his watch and shook his head. He marched over to the man holding the tablet. "All right, thank you for your care and diligence." He gently plucked the tablet from the worker's hands. "Out you go. Step lively." He shooed them away. "I'm not paying overtime."

McPhee clutched the tablet to his chest as he watched them exit the gallery. When they were gone, he held the tablet up for closer inspection. It was a remarkable piece. Priceless, really. But magic?

He rolled his eyes and inserted the tablet into its custom display. He stood back beside Ahkmenrah's sarcophagus and studied the piece from afar.

There was something about it though...

McPhee knew what it was. One of the tablet's movable tiles was slightly askew. He reached up and gently pushed the rogue tile. It lightly clicked into position. McPhee stood back and checked it again. Now it was perfect.

The museum director moved out of the display and headed toward the chamber's exit. The amber light from the setting sun painted the museum beyond the dark gallery. The director stopped near the exit and turned to take in the sight once more. Everything was just as it had been. It was as if the pharaoh and the Tablet of Ahkmenrah had never left.

McPhee smiled at his accomplishment. He spun on his heels and marched toward the exit with a spring in his step.

Suddenly, golden light flashed on the walls around him. McPhee skid to stop. Where was the light coming from? The sun had just set and ...

Dr. McPhee tightened his lips as he slowly spun around. When he saw the tablet, his eyes went wide and his mouth hung open.

"It does glow ..."